Dalton's Daughter

The Autobiography

of Sasha Wheaton

by

Virginia Carraway Stark

STARKLIGHT PRESS

Published by StarkLight Press

a Division of StarkLight Industries

1 Kala Road, Fraser Lake, B.C.

Canada

V0J 1S0

www.starklightpress.com

Copyright © StarkLight Press, 2014

Set in FreeSans 8/9/12/18/28

Printed by ~~IngramSpark~~. 48Hour Books

3

"Be thine own palace,

or the world's thy jail."

-John Donne.

Publisher's Foreword

Sasha Wheaton was always a bit of a mystery.

Her inner workings were knit up tighter than the accounts of Victorinus Wrought. From the beginning, it was obvious that Sasha had deeply powerful motives for her actions- she was given to fabulous gestures of kindness and compassion. She had profound reserves of strength both physical and psychological. While being an obviously sentimental and optimistic person, Sasha always surprised us at unexpected moments by showing a strength of command that would stop any shenanigans in its tracks. The motives for these actions, and the profound depths of her affection and loyalties, were consistently obscure.

Sasha was, therefore, the quintessential woman, and it would take her equal on the other side of the page to reveal the incredible complexity of Sasha's experience. The GAF Mainframe was devised originally as a playground for scientific hypotheticals, a repository for rollicking old fashioned space Adventure and a wry, satiric commentary on the technological human condition. Sasha's presence first in the infamous Detach Detachment, then in the life of the movers and shakers of the GAF universe, had always existed.

Like most womens' roles in a masculine and largely cutthroat environment, the reasons *why* Sasha were ineffable. She just was. She just did. She cropped up when you needed her in a story, and often when you didn't, and that was that. Sasha thus began as the caregiver of the GAF, the reliable motherly, big-sisterly figure.

With the realization that Verily Wrought had to join the GAF to personally counter-act his father's growing influence over the powerful military organization, the GAF universe was given its first real taste of deeper psychological subplot. Whereas before, the interior thoughts of the characters were given over to their machinations, their opinions on the worlds around them and the tools at their disposal, Sasha brought to us the first taste of true romance and psychological exposition. Her deep and abiding affection for a man she had never met tansformed from the crush she shared with most of the Galaxy to the first real look at not just the cogwheels of a GAF character's mind, but the thrumming, constant energies of the heart.

Breaking into that first fascinating glimpse of humanity in the GAF characters was a milestone. Of course it opened the GAF universe up to an entirely new audience who were more interested in the mechanisms of such a classic, Austenian relationship than the functioning of a Jump Drive. Figuring out the dynamics of such a polite romantic predicament in a world as relentless and invasive as the GAGA revealed itself to be equally fascinating in its construction as any patentable device. Sasha therefore supplied to the largely adolescent, masculine mindset of the GAF universe its first taste of the fascination provided by the fairer sex.

With the addition of Virginia Carraway Stark to the writing team of the GAF universe, the "Sasha situation" as it came to be called, began to unfold in earnest. With her uncanny acumen, Virginia was able to delve deeper into Sasha's motives, past and desires than any of us had before. Suddenly novellas of GAF adventures became full blown novels as the interior workings of the characters wound up informing most of the action already known in the GAF apocrypha. Short stories developed Sasha's reasons for what had once been obscure actions and reactions and fascinated us all. Other characters who had largely been two dimensional were able to bloom and develop into fascinating beings in their own right.

As the relationship between Sasha and Verily developed, so too did the entire GAF universe bloom in a springtime frenzy of feeling, emotional motivation and backstory. Sasha became thus the touchstone of the GAF, the jumping off point for many explorations into character and the embetterment of all involved- including the authors themselves.

In many ways, Sasha is now an embodiment of the multi-faceted goddess of Old Earth. This is a phenomenal accomplishment in the spiritual desert culture of the GAGA. Beginning as the nurturing but one-dimensional mother, Sasha grew to become the dynamo that sponsored the growth and maturity of every element in the GAF universe. She became muse, and finally partner and beloved queen of characters. In a universe that is acerbic, brutal and nearly devoid of the softer touch of the feminine energy, Sasha has single-handedly risen above its caustic qualities to engender those qualities throughout the Galaxy.

In the GAGA, she has become a cult favorite, a remarkable feat for a career military worker from a disregarded planet. In this outer realm of literary achievement, the telling of Sasha's story is perhaps the finest available discussion of the place of women, the goddess, and life as love in a consumerist world of technology. The honesty with which Virginia Carraway Stark narrates the savage events of Sasha's life will ring true with men and women alike. Speaking to the common, often hidden experience of half the population, she kindly opens the eyes of the other half to this intense, poignantly beautiful missing half of every story.

Here is Sasha's tale, the first part of it, anyway, in all it's harrowing, heart-wrenching and ultimately victorious glory. Enjoy.

Tony Stark,

Publisher and CEO,

StarkLight Press.

Prologue: Miracles

"Miracles are a retelling in small letters of the very same story which is written across the whole world in letters too large for some of us to see."

-C.S. Lewis

There is the smell of a baby and everyone knows what that smell is.

They may not be able to think of it right at first and I think it has a very different level of importance from one person to the next, but it is there, in the back of all our minds... that soft, unguarded warmth from their brains as they take in the brand new world around them. It's the smell of a young mind taking in all the newness of the world and learning what is expected of them. It is this newness that emanates from them with a pure radiating power that we interpret as smell.

The day my little sister was brought home I had little thoughts like that. I was little too and I sat on the couch with a pillow under my arm so that I could hold her neck up. I had seen her at the hospital. She was too small and she wasn't feeling well from the first time she came out of my mother. My daddy didn't like her, I could see that right from the start, and my mother didn't care much about her either, she would look down at her with eyes that looked dead and unseeing and that was the first time I noticed that it seemed like she was always taking handfulls of pills when her alarm on her Personal Device went off.

I held her in my arms and smelled the smell of new baby and couldn't believe that just a little bit before Anastasia hadn't existed in the world. I understood the word 'miracle' when I looked into her unfathomable dark blue eyes. I felt soft lips kiss my forehead and knew that somehow, it was the baby who had kissed me even as she sat unmoving in her arms. I lost my heart in that moment with her and swore in my heart and my mind to protect my miraculous sister always.

I failed her so often, but in the end I wouldnt' fail her and she knew all along. Anastasia always could read my heart.

11

Chapter One: Loss

"Have you ever lost someone you love and wanted one more conversation, one more chance to make up for the time when you thought they would be here forever? If so, then you know you can go your whole life collecting days, and none will outweigh the ones you wish you had back."

-Mitch Albom, 'For One More Day'.

It was a warm day in late spring but as I walked home from the bus I felt only the heavy pollution in the air and saw only the repitition of the sameness of the houses on the street. There was a weight across my brow that made me feel as though my vision was obstructed by my own eyelids and a dull fist of worry sat in my solar plexus.

The worry had started hours ago. Well, actually it had started with a sudden terror that had flooded me and left me feeling a need to run home, despite the fact that getting home without the bus from school was virtually impossible with the various checkpoints and fencing that only authorized vehicles could pass through.

The panic had then snapped shut and the dull heaviness had replaced it. It was as though someone had flipped a breaker box in my mind and shut the panic down. I knew who that someone was: Anastasia.

Walking home from the bus stop I clutched my holo-tablet to my chest and hummed Glen Miller to myself. As always when I hummed Glen Miller. I heard Stasia's soft sweet voice chime in with me, singing the words in her pure, guileless way. Her voice was muted, far away, but I was relieved to hear it. With the panic and the sudden clamping down on it, from her end, not from my end, I had feared the worst.

The attached rows of houses were white and grey and slate grey. They had small yards, about four by six feet in size out front but most had larger yards out the back and it was rare that there wouldn't be an illegal garden or chicken hutch as well. A railed balcony ran the length of each block of houses. Doors were individualized with planters of peas or plastic flowers or welcome mats ranging from classy to witty. The veranda that ran along the block of houses was quite small as well but nearly everyone had a chair or two to sit on and maybe a table to have a jar of iced Kaffee, the legalized chemical version of coffee that the poor drank. Only the rich with access to the black market would ever taste real coffee.

I didn't even realize there was a difference between Kaffee and Coffee. Everyone I knew drank Kaffee and the slight chemical buzz derived from it I was told was an augmented version of what caffeine caused in the system. It would be a long time and far away from here before I would taste the delight of real coffee and in very different company then the people behind my own identical door.

The veranda was a social networking opportunity as well as a place to get some fresh air. It was where we all went to get the latest gossip and news that the holo-vison wouldn't tell you and that we shouldn't have been telling each other for that matter, either. Today it was deserted. A lone pitcher of Lemon-fresh drink stood abandoned on an ornate plastic table that had been moulded and painted to look like wrought iron. It was thick with particles from being left out uncovered.

Theresa and Stacy went into their neighbouring doors across the street and down the way. Their voices had been quiet or perhaps they hadn't spoken as they walked back from the bus and their footfalls had been nearly silent. It was only the thudding of their screen doors that had let me know that I wasn't alone on the street after all.

Still humming 'Don't Sit Under the Apple Tree' as I put my hand on the latch for my own screen door, Anastasia's voice cut out abruptly.

I opened the door to the sound of the holovision playing loudly in the living room. The foyer of my house was very small, the inner door barely had room to open up into it and then you had to shut it again in order to open any of the other doors or even get into the closet.

I was still attempting to close the outside door when my mom opened the door leading from the kitchen. I squeezed around the outside door and closed it so that she could get through. I took one look at her face and didn't like what I saw. The panic I felt earlier that day rose up again, mom's make up was slightly blurred around her eyes as though she had fallen asleep and cried a little while she slept. Her eyes wore the slack dreamy look of someone who had taken twice her medication before her nap and woke feeling much less of whatever had made her cry.

"I made your favourite for dinner, Sasha."

She smiled at me, her eyes never making eye contact with mine while she did.

"Where's Anastasia?" I blurted through lips that felt swollen and numb. Her eyes darted down and to the left and she turned in a little circle and went back into the kitchen, shutting the door behind her with a tiny 'snicking' noise. The holovision continued to blare from behind the door to the living room. I put my shoes into the closet and went into the living room with a dreamy feeling in my head of impending doom.

Daddy was sitting in his reclining chair and watching three holographinc three dimensional girls give a rowsing cheer calling for manly men to buy more Puddin' Hots. The ad was typical of the sort that appealed this time of day and it

15

encouraged manly men to 'put it to them while the Puddin' was Hot'. I swallowed the lump in my throat. The power of the man sitting in his E-Z Boy recliner that was too big for the room was profound over me. He had feared Anastasia since she had been born, he and mother both had, but at least mother loved her as much as she knew how.

"Hi, Daddy," I said through a sick, forced smile. He looked at me with eyes deliberately dimmed to hide his triumph. Where oh where was 'Stasia?

I didn't say the question screaming behind my eyes that stung with unshed tears. I could only hide them and the thudding of my heart in my chest so much. She wasn't here. Anastasia wasn't here.

"How was school?"

"It was good. I passed my chemistry test."

"That's good. The boss said we would all have dinner soon. It's your big chance, Sash."

"Where's 'Stasia?" I blurted.

I didn't want to hear about my big chance to work at the nuclear power plant. Terra 65F, more commonly known as Dalton, was designated an energy planet. Dalton had been discovered by one of the thousands of probes that the Galactic Association of Globes and Asteroids or GAGA, used to expand its empire and was named for the scientist who had discovered its commercial worth and had it designated, Albert Dalton. He had discovered my planet to be a rich reserve of natural uranium and phosphorous. Colonists had been selected to come and work at the factories and plants that Verily Munitions built and for five generations now Dalton had been an inhabited planet.

Where there were uranium deposits, uranium enriching facilities were built and nearby nuclear power plants were built like the one less then a mile east from where I lived. Except for the parking lot, there were rows of houses just like mine built right up to the chainlink fence that surrounded the Nuke plant. Enormous high voltage powerlines ran radially out from the plant, one set touched the edge of the alley behind my house.

The power lines went to a different type of factory where it was transformed with patented Verily technology into large concentrated batteries that were used in munitions and war torn areas to fortify the GAGA troops. As it was pointed out to me daily in school, it was good to know that we were helping out the good guys.

In five generations we had successfully mined and refined 12% of Dalton's mass and exported it off the planet. It was a pretty good statistic, most energy planets shot for 8% in that amount of time but I guess our first settlers must have brought some genes for over achieving with them.

The cooling towers that loomed in the east had been with me my whole life. They towered over the nearby plateau to the north and it would be a long time on other planets before I would ever learn to see a sunrise without cooling towers silhouetted in it as natural.

Once we had mined about 45% of the planet's mass its orbit would no longer be able to be sustained, even with Wrought Satellites to hold it in place. Even then, my whole world depended on Verily Wrought and his father and I said or thought their names fifty or sixty times a day just in the course of going to school and cooking dinner, or washing my hair with Verily High Resolution Shine Shampoo.

Daddy looked at me, his face was a mask of sorrow. ``I`m sorry, Sasha. We all loved Anastasia very much, but there was a problem with her today. I was at work but I came home as quickly as I could, it was too late...``

"What happened?" I was crying now. Let him see. He held out his arms to me. I went to him, reluctant but happy for any contact, even his. He put his footstool down and I sat on his lap while he stroked my hair.

"She started to have a seizure. The doctor said that she probably died of a stroke."

"Probably?"

"Probably. We'll never really know, I signed the agreement for her body to be incinerated, we were lucky for every day with her... you know, when she was born the doctors said she probably wouldn't live to be six, she made it to fourteen. Fourteen goddamn years. She was a fighter, sweety. My sweet Sasha. We still have each other, don't we. You've always been Daddy's girl."

His hand stroking my hair was hot and dry. It stopped stroking my hair and he cupped the shape of my head with his whole hand and pushed it against his chest firmly. After a moment he started to stroke my hair again. I was facing the bookshelf, it was a small one but the antique collection of books on it was one of the things that was a family heirloom. It had been on Dalton for five generations now and would leave when the planet had been so thoroughly mined that it could no longer support life, assuming there were any Wheatons still on the planet to take it, that is. Daddy was still talking, telling me about how lucky we had been to have had 'Stasia, but she was never quite right, was she. We were still a family though.

I looked at the spines of the books to escape his words and his false soothings, justification for his joy that Anastasia had died and he had me all to himself now. No Annie to protect me from night time visits from Daddy now. It would be just like when I was four all over again, just like before 'Stasia had been born and she had used her special ways to save me for fourteen years from sleepless nights of terror of the boogeyman.

I found a book with my eyes, it was the one about

19

Camelot and Arthur and his knights. That place, back on earth, the first Terra, a place that I had never seen and knew nothing about except from books and pictures. It was a place so far away in scope, with rolling hills where there were no buildingslike the ones that surrounded me. There would be trees everywhere, not just one every sixth house, but trees that didn't have fences around them... and there would be the Lords and Ladies.

In my mind I was, of course, Guinivere. What girl could resist playing at being her? The king, the greatest king in the history of our galaxy, and he wanted me. Our love was pure... too pure, and it was the passion of Lancelot that would be my downfall...

Trapped by my imagining I ran into a wayward memory- Anastisia jumping out from behind the door of our shared room, she had a play sword and she spoke, I always remembered when she spoke. Daddy and I had just had a fight he had been yelling at me outside the door.

"Dragon! I Lancelot, Sister."

She was slaying the dragon with her sword, the deadly lizard that was our father. She was Lancelot and I was Guenevire. She spoke so little and very few people understood the words she spoke. When she spoke to me, or even just looked at me, her whole story was in my mind as clearly as

20

though I had read it in a book or watched it on holo-vision. In my memory, i smiled through my tears (Daddy could always make me cry) and said, ``My hero!"

We had played Lancelot and Guenevire for the rest of the evening. We were hunting a crystal that, once found, would keep all dragons from the Kingdom for all time. We would give it as a gift to Merlin and he would set it in his staff.

I guess we never found the crystal. The dragon had killed Lancelot and it was only a matter of time before he ravished the damsel Guenevire. Merlin is never around when you need him.

Daddy's hand had moved from my hair to my back where his fingers traced the outline of my bra strap. I jumped out of his lap and wiped the tears from my eyes. I fled up the stairs and could hear Daddy humming the theme song for Puddin' Hots as I did.

As I have mentioned, our house was very small. It was actually, of course, a townhouse, but on Terra 65F it was about the only type of house built and so we just called it a house. Even the bigwigs who worked at the nuke plant rarely had their very own house. Energy planets just didn't warrant a whole lot of luxury. I ran up the narrow stairway, it was so narrow that if two people met on it one of them would have to go up or down to let the other pass. There were two bedrooms upstairs and the bathroom. One was my parents and one belonged to me and 'Stasia. It had a set of bunkbeds, Anastasia's toy box, a small closet where our dresser was as well, a night stand and my desk for schoolwork in it. That was about all there was room for but it had enough space in the center of the room for Annie to play with her dolls or to stretch out and colour and lay out some of her other pictures for comparison. There was no space for a desk for 'Stasia to do school work which worked out all right as she would never go to school.

My Daddy lied about a lot of things, but he didn't lie about what the doctors had said about Anastasia when she was born. She was unlikely to survive until she was six. She was born autistic and with alterations (what they call mutations) in her brain that made survival dubious. They didn't understand the alterations, they didn't care to investigate them, too many children had them to bother and each child had a different alteration so investigating for one child would prove nothing.

I didn't want them to look at Anastasia's alterations. Whether it was something in her chemistry, or something in her brain, or just the nature of her spirit, what she lacked in I.Q. she made up for in her other talents. She could do things, she could move things, she put on music without standing up or saying a word. Even when she had been a baby, her favourite toys would jump off the ground and into her crib. The first time Daddy had come into our room after Annie had come home from the hospital she had started to murmur. She didn't cry. Not ever, not once that I knew her even as a baby did she cry.

We didn`t have a bunkbed then, my desk wasn`t there either as I was too young to need one. Where it would be was Annie`s crib and hung from the ceiling was our entire solar system. At the sound of the murmurings from Annie`s crib, the planets began to fall. They didn't just fall though, they were thrown. I could see them by the glow of the night light. They were thrown right at daddy who cried out 'ow' when the first one hit him on the crown of his head.

Then they were picked up from the floor and thrown again. Bam, fifteen planets and their moons pelting him on the head and in the face. He clambered off of me, he was terrified. Oddly, I wasn't. I sat up and pulled the covers around me. Baby Anastasia raised her hand in the air and the planets rose as one, she was going to hit him all at once with them. They weren't that heavy but I knew that Daddy would go from frightened to angry in a hurry if he was actually hurt.

"Anastasia, don't," Her little fist was still in the air, her eyes blinking in that unfocused way that new borns have. She lowered her fist and put it in her mouth instead. The planets fell to the ground but Daddy hadn't been content to leave well enough alone... what had followed had been much worse, but in the end Anastasia had stopped the bedroom visits from Daddy.

Nothing was said about Stasia's abilities for ages. Advanced psychic powers weren't entirely unknown to happen, but it was an alteration and alterations were bad. Many children would have special talents and then they would die, usually from a stroke or a seizure. Their minds were special and they held more spirit then a normal body, but their bodies were flawed and would fail them.

The special talents could be extremely frightening. Rows of houses had been burned down by accidents caused by fire starters. Mind readers who drove those around them insane... the rumours were as disparate as the talents.

There were also rumours of succesful talents, and the troops who wore all black and drove the black turtle tanks to take them away to where they could be understood, monitored and utilized. That was what happened to the ones who learned how to control their talents. Nobody ever saw them again so all the rest was rumours and supposition.

That was why nobody talked about Anastasia. If you loved someone or related to their situation, you just didn't talk about things that could hurt them. I knew other boys and girls who went to Stasia's daycare and could do little things. Nothing like 'Stasia, but they could do these things and nobody ever talked about them. If raising their hand made their toy spin on the floor, you gently lowered their hand and told them that wasn't a good thing to do. Then you found something else to entertain them.

That was what I wanted to do, was to work at a daycare group with children and to be with Anastasia every day. I didn't want to work at the nuclear plant even though it was better pay and better benefits. I wanted to be with 'Stasia.

I got to the top of the stairs and turned into our bedroom. I could see immediately that it was just my bedroom now.

Our bedroom had been sanitized. I walked into it and all signs of Annie had been eradicated. Her toy box was gone, her blankets and pillow were gone, even her mattress pad had been removed. Her clothes had been taken out of the closet and the dresser. Her crayon pictures removed from the wall.

There was nothing left of her. I closed the door and sat on the floor with my back leaning against it. She was really gone.

I wondered who had cleaned the bedroom, maybe mother had done it before she took more pills to dull her pain. Maybe it had been a vestige of her caring, since 'Stasia was dead now, maybe Mother felt safe enough to show some sort of strange version of affection by removing Anastasia's things. The more I thought about it, the more I realized that removing a child's things only hours after her death was weird. It didn't fit with either of my parents and what I knew of them.

I noticed a red, half used crayon that whoever had cleaned the bedroom had left behind. I picked it up and smiled at it, it felt like Anastasia and I was frankly surprised that the feel of her didn't make me cry again. I felt happy and content.

The way she always made me feel. Safe.

"Roses are RED, Sister." Her voice, in my mind. Her voice, as clear as though she were in the room with me. I tried to remember when she had told me that, Roses are RED, but I couldn't recall, and I always recalled when she spoke.

I put the crayon in the top drawer of our dresser. I needed some air. I went downstairs to go out into the backyard. The door to go outside is through the kitchen so I had to go back down the stairs, through the living room where Daddy smiled at me in a smug way and through the miniscule foyer back into the kitchen. Mother was still in the kitchen.

She was standing motionless by the counter.

"Mother?" I walked up to her cautiously. She felt brittle to me. "Are you all right?"

She turned to me, she had been crying since I saw her last. I put a hand on her shoulder. She shook her head, no, she wasn't all right. She had been standing over our families instant dinners. She was trying to 'make' mine and Anastasia's favourite dinner. It was something I had invented one evening to please 'Stasia and I was nuts about it too. Mother and Daddy thought it was good but didn't like how much work it was to make.

It was really very decadent as it was one and a half meal a piece. You took a mushroom pasta linguini meal and you put the mushroom sauce, pretty much congealed mushroom soup, onto the ham and fresh vegetable meal. I realized that Mother couldn't figure out how to make the meal for three people as it meant that half of one of the extra opened meals was wasted. It worked to make the meal for two people or four people, but not for three.

"I don't know what to do." She sobbed. I nodded in understanding.

"I'm really not hungry, Mother. Just open the two ham dinners and one mushroom dinner. That'll work out just fine."

She inhaled deeply with relief, grateful to be told what to do and to be offered a solution to her dilema. I went past her and out the door. I didn't know if I would be able to eat tonight or not but I thought that I would likely just pull the tab on a Puddin' Hot if I wanted something. They were my favourite comfort food of the time and what I considered to be Victorinus Wrought's, owner of Wrought Industries, greatest invention.

Puddin' Hots came in all flavours, butterscotch, strawberry, chocolate, banana... pretty much any fruit or sweet thing. All you do to eat one is pull the tab on it and it releases a chemical reaction that freshly cooks and warms the puddin' (which is really more like a sauce cake then pudding) and its ready for your personal enjoyment.

I went out into the back yard. It was one of the areas that we had for our personal living space that actually had room in it. It had an illegal garden in it that me and my mother tended and it gives us all of our fresh vegetables and herbs. It's a job of work growing anything but we do it. We have to grow the plants under plastic awnings that let in sun but not rain as the rain tends to eat holes in all the vegetation if it's a bad day. We run the water through a filter and that gets rid of most of the alpha particles that damage leaves and we just don't eat the ones that look too funky. Too many alterations.

It's a nice backyard. One of the limbs of our neighbour's tree sticks over the high wooden fence and Daddy put up a swing on it for me and 'Stasia. It's my favourite place to be. I sat on the swing and gave myself a little push. I still couldn't believe that Anastasia was dead. I closed my eyes and relived the feeling that I had had at school. That sudden panic and fear... it wasn't sorrow, that had come later... and it had the sensation of being rended in half, not of being killed though.

I reached out in my mind for the tenuous connection that still existed where the strong connection had been before this afternoon- it was still there. Was it in my imagination? I didn't believe anything was in my imagination with Anastasia, I had had too much physcial proof since she had come into my lilfe and I respected her too much then to put doubts and fears onto 'Stasia.

I was sure that she was still alive. She was somewhere and she wasn't very happy, but she wasn't in immediate danger either. I thought of black turtle trucks and shuddered. How could I find out if my feeling was true or not? Mother and Daddy's story made a lot less sense then the trucks coming for 'Stasia. It was naive of me to think that they were above finding a way out from having to put up with Anastasia anymore. There were rewards for reporting 'dangerous' anomolous persons, or D.A.P.'s as they were casually referred to. I didn't want to believe it could have been mother or daddy and so I turned my feeling of anger and sorrow out at the world at large and let myself cry quietly but with large hitchings in my chest and tears so bitter and salty they burned my cheeks where they ran.

I was nearly cried out, and I'm not sure how much time had passed as I sat on the swing, but my legs and feet had fallen asleep and so I wiggled them around while I wiped my face on the edge of my pink t-shirt and tried not to do or think anything that might set me off again.

Then my second favourite person in the whole world came to see me and made my day. The fence between our place and our neighbours isn't all that secure in places along the bottom and that was where Penny pushed aside a board and came to see me. She snuffled my hand, put her paws on my chest and licked my face clean of salty tears.

Rhoda opened the gate that adjoined our yards and

came huffing and panting under her large girth over to see me. Penny was Rhoda's incredibly illegal Pitbull. I loved Penny more then I loved anyone other then Anastasia. I picked Penny up on the swing and hugged her hard. It helped so much.

Rhoda was ostensibly on disablity due to 'injury' received through working at the nuke plant. In truth she was (what I thought of at the time) a master of the black market. I would learn later on that she was barely a dabbler but she constantly impressed me with her gift for getting obscure and illegal merchandise. Penny was an example of this. Where on earth had Rhoda come across a puppy on Dalton? Not just a puppy, but a pit bull puppy? They were considered to be illegal weapons and if anyone ever tattled on Rhoda she would not just be fined but also imprisoned.

Rhoda had kept Penny for seven years now. I could still remember the first time I saw her, she was a squirming little puppy and the first living animal I had ever seen. It wouldn't be until I left Dalton that I would see another living animal. Energy planets have very strict laws in place, way stricter then most planets, although there are exceptions that are far stricter. Nobody ever tattled on Rhoda, at least not while I knew her.

Rhoda was in her own orbit, and was large enough to possibly have her own gravitational pull. I never met anyone who didn't like her. She was like Santa and the easter bunny and a grandmother all rolled into one. She was beaming her usual smile but I could see that her eyes were sad for me. I avoided her gaze, and focused on loving and hugging Penny.

Other than the red crayone, it was the first thing all day that made me feel like I wasn't drowning in sorrow or panic.

Rhoda knew what had happened. I could see that from my furtive side glances at her face. It made sense, she would have seen some sort of kerfuffle. She was the only one in our neighbourhood who would likely have been around to see it, everyone worked and there wouldn't have been anyone around to see.

A discrepency in my theory swam into my sight. Anastasia should have been at the daycare today. If she was at the daycare, how would Rhoda known about the turtle trucks or an ambulance? It was like our bedroom being cleaned of all of Anastasia's things, it just didn't fit the story. The knowledge of my loss was on her face though, she knew that Anastasia was gone and had brought Penny to comfort her.

"I came over to show you something, my dear!" Her eyes were still sad for me, but there was something else as well, genuine excitement.

I smiled, just a little. Rhoda and Penny had that affect on me. "What is it?"

"The apple tree has set."

It took me a minute to understand and then a minute more to believe her.

Every sixth house has a tree in the back yard. It was an initiative that was started thirty years ago to quell a movement that complained about the dearth of fruit on the planet. Each tree planted was a different sort of fruit tree, apple, peach, plum or cherry. They alternate all the way down. The person who has the tree shares their bounty in exchange for the vegetables and other things that other people have. It was a great gift and really great since it was legal fruit.

I should specify that it isn't actually illegal to grow vegetables, it's just illegal to own or plant seeds. Of course, the seeds must be obtained and planted in order to grow a garden so you can draw some conclusions from the existence of fresh vegetables in a yard as they aren't sold as seedlings on our planet and they are also illegal to import. Fortunately there isn't a specific police force or government agency to enforce these rules so it's really just something that's trotted out every so often if you get into trouble with really really the wrong bigwig. It's such a rare thing to get into trouble over and everyone has one, it's just not something to really talk about or acknowledge.

So, Rhoda's fruit tree was great. All the fruit trees were great! There was just one problem that the community planners had either failed to take into account or had thought of and had a good laugh at. The fruit trees were imported by Verily Green

Growers as saplings but they required pollination and the few winged insects that had existed on Dalton before the first colonists arrived had been extinct for ages now. There was no way for the trees to be pollinated.

We are all still colonists, even though we are fifth generation. We came up with a solution for the problem. Every spring when the blossoms come out we have spring setting parties. They happen at different times depending on the fruit and the variety but the owners of each tree have learned how to tell when its time for a party without fail. I knew that Rhoda's party was supposed to be next week, we all dressed up with yellow and black fuzzy antenna headbands, the antennas came out in little springs and bounced about while we took the long telescoping sticks with special soft sponges on the end and gently pollinated each blossom.

The party wasn't until next week, so how on earth had they set?

"Do you want to come have a look at the blossoms?" Rhoda was bouncing on her feet she was so excited. For the moment, I forgot about Anastasia and followed Rhoda through the gate with Penny following at my heels.

I looked up at the apple tree, its leaves were gently fuzzy on the bottom and the blossoms were stained pink. I took hold of a small branch at face height and gently shook it, the blossom held. I inspected the base of the blossom, a tiny swelling had formed already. Rhoda wasn't kidding the blossoms had set. I took hold of another branch and pulled back my hand in surprise at a strange vibration that took hold of my fingers, I removed my hand and the vibration stopped. I had heard it in my ears as well and after a minute it started up again. Rhoda watched my face expectantly. I looked at her and then back at the branch. I put my face close up by the branch. Something yellow and orange with a little black head and wings looked up at me. I looked at Rhoda again. "Is that-"

"A real life honey bee? Yes!" Rhoda clasped her hands over her large bosom and jumped up on her tiptoes excitedly. I bought them... a whole hive of them!"

"But how? The air here isn't rated for flying insects!"

"These are Buzz-bees. Genetically enhanced bees designed by Dr. Buxbie. He takes orders and designs bees for planets who can no longer support such things."

"Are they legal?" I asked the answer mentally and stopped the words before they got over my tongue. Of course they wouldn't be legal! Genetically enhanced oranisms were never legal to import unless you were an industrial company with large resources to ensure that they were compatible with existing lifeforms. It was absurd since Dalton didn't have any insects or animals. Regardless, Rhoda could be in big trouble for this, bigger the the trouble with Penny who had at least been bred locally on Dalton.

Rhoda beckoned for me to follow her and led me to a white plastic box that she had attached to the back of her house. Penny walked over the the hive which was buzzing merrily and wagged her tail at me. She was happy something had made Rhoda so happy, but then, who knows how much dogs like Penny can understand. Rhoda lifted up the lid of the hive, several bees landed on her hands and crawled on them. I recoiled a bit.

"Don't bees sting? Are these ones fixed so they don't?" I watched in facination as a bee landed on Rhoda's face and walked around on her forehead.

"Oh, these guys still sting, Buzz-bees are made to survive and stinging helps them protect themselves."

"Aren't you afraid?"

Rhoda laughed and shooed the bees off of her hands and back to the hive and closed the lid.

"No, what's to be afraid of. These guys might sting me a bit but only if I scare them or get too clumsy with them. Look here, sweetheart, look how they make it up to me." She took a small jar from beside her back steps and held it out to me. It was amber and gold in the sunlight.

She opened the jar and dipped her finger into it and popped it into her mouth and then held the jar out to me. I followed her lead and smiled broadly.

"Real honey!"

She nodded excitedly and pushed the jar into my hands. "For you, sweetheart, to make the days ahead a bit sweeter."

My first thought was to share it it with Anastasia. Realizing I had no one I could share it with was a fresh punch in my liver and tears came back to my eyes. Dusk was spreading out from the east between the cooling tower and the world was stained red from the large sun of Dalton setting. Our dusk always dyed the world into colors of blood, but tonight it seemed real and true to me, it seemed like my world was blood and death. My eyes hurt with shed and unshed tears. Rhoda hugged me to her warm softness in an encompassing embrace. I felt it then, the fact that the spritual ties that had bound me to Anastasia were strained or gone. She was gone. Honey filled my mouth with sweetness different from the chemical sweetness to which I was accustomed.

Rhoda let me cry until her bosom and armpit were covered in my tears. She whispered in my ear.

"I saw it all, I saw it all. Your Dad brought her home, she was sound asleep on his shoulder... then the turtle trucks came... he called them, Sasha, sweet Sasha, it could only have been your dad... if she had been awake they wouldn't have dared take her, she would have stopped them... they have drugs they give her kind, to make them sleep, drugs that are illegal unless the military issues them... I'm so sorry, my dear, but they took her, soldiers dressed in black... she was still asleep, not dead but asleep... I'm so sorry, if I had been braver perhaps I could have woken her, but you know I'm not brave, and I have Penny to think about... Penny and the bees... I'm sorry my dear, but you know that I'm not brave..."

The litany continued and the only words that rung with me then were, 'not dead but asleep', 'it could only have been your dad', and 'drugs they give *her kind*'. I felt dizzy and Rhoda helped me into her house and sat me on her small couch.

Her house was as small as our house but with only Rhoda and Penny in it and the holovision turned off, it seemed much larger then our cramped house, the mirror of this one only right next door. I could hear small sounds coming through the wall from my own house. Someone clunking in the kitchen and the holovision coming tinnily through the wall. Daddy had the game turned up too loud. Rhoda let me cry myself out and Penny licked my cheeks. What did I think about Rhoda's revelations?

They weren't exactly revelations to me, I had felt that Anastasia was't dead after all. I had known that Daddy had wanted her gone for years now... I couldn't imagine what had made him decide then to report her and have her taken and I never found out what did. Perhaps there was a commercial on holo about the importance of reporting irregular persons, or maybe 'Stasia had said something to him that had cut him.

It was immaterial and all that mattered was that he had betrayed his own children for selfish gain. I'm sure he justfied it with the same language that Rhoda justified for her own cowardice . I loved Penny and the honey from the bees as well, but there was no justification. Anastasia was special, is special, and she deserved to be protected by the people in her life. It's always the ones who deserve to be protected who are betrayed. Worthless people like my Daddy have nothing to be betrayed about, they are null and void and serve only to null and void others.

Others like Anastasia, but also others like myself.

Back in my own bedroom that night, the door creaked open and Daddy was standing there, then he was under the covers with me and now he didn't bother being kind. He cried acid salty tears that burned on my skin as he bemoaned all the year he had lost with me and loved me as though I were his wife. Daddy had what he wanted, it was all betrayal and all his gain.

The vulnerable shouldn't be at the mercy of the stronger, that was part of what made me decide to join the GAF later on. That was what I told the recruiting sergeant when the time came and I paid the fee to take the officer's exam. I filled that in, the answer to question number one.

Number one: Why are you interested in becoming a commanding officer in the Galactic Armed Forces?

I want to join the GAF because I believe that the vulnerable should not be at the mercy of the stronger and I will use all force to ensure this. I also want off of Dalton ASAP.

I think the answer I gave was fairly immaterial since I found out later on that it was more about the fee and less about the answers you gave but my answer got me through a lot of dark nights after I enlisted.

That first dark night with no Anastasia and with Daddy in my bed, I couldn't imagine any sort of future. I thought about killing myself. It wasn't a dramatic sort of thought, it was quiet and constructive. I wondered about methods and itinerized how I could kill myself with minimum discomfort and mess. I thought about my mother's pills and wondered how many I would have to take and if I would fall asleep like *she* did every night, like she was right now and closed off to the loss of one daughter and the violation of the other. I wondered if I would get sick and throw up before I took enough to die. I wondered if

I could stab myself in the throat with a kitchen knife. Those were the thoughts I thought to try to forget about the man/monster slavering and stabbing on top of me.

The next day I got up, I could barely walk and I was bruised on my breasts and shoulders and thighs. Daddy wasn't gentle about the things he wanted.

I went to school, glad for the distraction of the work. The yes/good, no/bad bear came out time after time as I plowed through my tests and quiz work. Most of our schol work was done singularly on our holoputers. The school bear came out for each question answered. He walked in from the horizon, starting small and growing bigger and holding a sign on a two-by-four. As he came closer to the observer he would look at you speculatively and then turn the sign one way or the other as a response to the input you had given. Either yes/good! Or no/bad.

The school system on Dalton was said, on Dalton, to be exceedingly good. The rest of the galaxy didn't think the same way.

I would have spent all day and all night at school if I could have, but of course, I had to go home at the end of the day, home and to Daddy.

It was Anastasia that kept me from killing myself those first days. I could feel her put the brakes on those thoughts. It

40

sounds crazy to say, but if you believe that she could stop Daddy from getting at me all those years, you have to believe that she could stop me from doing something that I didn't want to do anyhow.

I didn't want to kill myself. Everyday that I woke up and Daddy had gone back to his own bed and I could hear the speakers outside playing the sounds of birds singing and the sun was shining, and sometimes I would see a bee on my window ledge or wave at Penny who liked to chew on various items in the backyard, I would feel glad that I was still alive. I would shower and get his smell out of my nose and have breakfast and not think about how much more time I had every morning now that I didn't have to make breakfast for 'Stasia and help her with her socks and shoes. So much extra time and so much less love.

The walk to school was a delusion of a real and natural planet. It was with the sound of birds that would never fly in Dalton's skies and under a plum tree that would have to be pollinated by studens that I said 'yes' to Victor Lathen when he asked me to go to prom. It was the end of the school year and I had refused to look into any job in a serious way. I found thoughts of the future to put me into dark places too quickly and easily and avoided them. I knew that this was idiocy, the sooner I could get a career path the sooner I could apply for my own housing alotment and the sooner I could shut the door forever on daddy.

It wasn't daddy that kept me from a new job, it was the

thought of losing the last whispers of Anastasia that kept me from persuing my own future. I didn't want to get into the nuclear plant, I didn't want to take care of disadvantaged children with autism or other aberrations. I didn't want anything. When I went to prom, daddy was very angry with me.

He was angry when he heard I had a date, he was angry when mother brought me home a midnight blue dress, he was furious when Vic came to the door to walk me to the bus.

At the dance, Vic and I danced and I drank from the metal flask he gave me, watching me avidly as I did so. My stomach burned and I was surprised to feel the knot of pain that lived with me all the time relax a little. I asked for the flask again and Vic elbowed one of his buddies as I drank it back as quickly as the burning allowed.

Underneath the plum tree I lay under Vic passively and watched the stars I could see twinkle between the branches above my head. Vic threw up my skirt and explored where he wanted. He was rough compared to some, but his touch seemed kind to me then. He touched me timorously, eagerly, scared that I would wake up from my drunken fugue and tell him to stop. I didn't even know that you could tell someone 'no' when they did things to you. It would always be the bear with the sign for years to come. If I said 'yes' I was GOOD! and 'no' I was BAD.

I was GOOD! For Vic and the next morning I returned home on the bus feeling oddly happy with myself. Vic hadn't bruised me and I had felt something like pleasure from his fumblings, I had at the very least been happy to be GOOD! For someone who wasn't Daddy.

It wasn't Vic to tore my prom dress and it wasn't Vic who left me unable to walk for three days after prom. It was Daddy in the early morning hours who did that.

I hadn't had my period for three months by the time prom came. I didn't know that there was necessarily a problem with that, lots of girls didn't get a period in their whole life. The school was doing the final breeding viability tests when they found out that I was pregnant. Only I knew that there had been no one four months ago except daddy.

I walked away from school after I was told about the baby inside of me. The baby who was a monster. It wasn't my fault most likely, they said. They said that it was most likely an environmental difficulty but that I had to come to the hospital and tell them the details of the parentage and allow them to remove the horror that was growing in me. I didn't believe them that it was a non-viable, I asked to be given a picture. The blonde doctor's mouth twitched into a frown and she looked at me so kindly I nearly cried and didn't take the print out she handed me. I took it from her and saw the child, the thing that was all the horror that Anastasia had been accused of and wasn't. This was a demon inside of me and 'Stasia had been an angel.

I walked all the way to the enormous concrete barrier that protected our compound from the undesireable elements of Dalton. Elements like criminals, industrial pollution and black marketeers. I didn't have the paperwork to go through and cameras watched me look through the bars that kept me safely locked up. My belly had been growing. I hadn't noticed in my grief. I hadn't cared when my pants grew too tight and had just asked mother for new ones.

I glimpsed the world through the bars for several hours and slowly a plan started to form in rough hash marks in my mind. Would it work? It might, and if it didn't, I would kill myself and the monster growing inside of me. The monster that wouldn't survive an hour in the air if it survived to full term. Anastasia couldn't stop me from this, this time I would want to kill myself. If I had to go to the hospital and have it removed, have them all know who the father was.

Daddy's behavior was a sure sign of aberration. It was not 'cool' with the nuclear bosses that many of their workers had severe personality problems. It was important to be perceived as wholesome and safe by the company. Daddy's behavior wouldn't have surpised many of his co-workers who had perversions of their own, but any such perversions brought to light would result in summary firing. Daddy would be sent to the far side of the wall. I might be sent there too if the right person decided to send me there. It was all down to what would look best for the company. What would be easiest. Whatever happened, I wouldn't be living in this compound for long and life was through these gates and it was all in daddy's hands.

Daddy was watching the holovision in his e-z boy when I came home. I walked into the living room and slammed the door quietly behind me.

"Daddy, we have to talk. No. You have to listen."

My eyes glimmered and my thighs were shaking with the fear of my ultimatum. All that kept me from going to pieces was the detached part of my mind that didn't want him to say 'yes' (GOOD!), that wanted to get mother's bottle of pills and be done with the whole sorry mess of my life.

I told Daddy about my appointment the next day, I told him in the vaguest of terms and without meeting his eyes about the aberration of the foetus inside me. Even when told vaguely he pulled away from me in distaste at the thought of what my body, our body's had made together. I told him that I knew about Anastasia, that I knew about the reward money the government had paid him and that I wanted it. All of it, or I would keep my appointment tomorrow and tell them every detail.

My eyes spat fire when I told him that part and I lifted my trembling chin defiantly at him. This part was all bluff and I was drawing on all of my rage to keep the lie out of my eyes. He couldn't know that I would rather he killed me then to keep that appointment. He had to believe me.

He did believe me. He turned into an old, defeated man before my eyes and it was his knees that trembled, it was he who staggered backward into his e-z boy and clutched his head.

He left the house immediately after telling me I could take his and mother's travel cases from the closet in their room and take anything I wanted from the house. He didn't ask me where I would go or what I would do when the money ran out, he just asked me repeatedly to swear I would 'get rid of it' without anyone finding out. I had surprised him into a state of shock and I don't think he realized exactly that I was leaving Dalton. He didn't really think that no matter what, I would have to explain where the mutant miscarriage had gone to. It was a criminal act to dispose of 'hazardous biological material' as it was euphemistically called. I had a plan and Daddy didn't care what it was so long as he didn't get into trouble for it. He didn't want to have to face the consequences of his crimes but in the end, women must always face the crimes that men have the luxury of turning away from.

I packed my things and some of the books on the shelf, only the ones that wouldn't make me too sad though. I ran back up the narrow stairs and grabbed the red crayon I found. I put everything into one suitcase and waited anxiously for Daddy to come home, hoping mother's work would keep her away so we wouldn't have to deal with any more questions.

Daddy and I had become 'we' in our conspiracy and I detested myself for wanting him to come home with what I needed to survive. I wrung my hands and looked out the front window.

He finally came home with a large envelope stuffed full of money, it was everything from their savings account, everything except what they needed to pay or their immediate expenses and bills. I know because he also showed me his bank statement. He had produced it to me with the air of a martyr but I had nodded in satisfaction when I read it. I wanted to leave them both bereft. Mother for not helping either of her daughters and daddy for... well, you know, for everything.

He had also gotten the papers required to attach to my i.d. So that I could leave the compound and go into the city proper. I don't know how he got thoses papers but I suspect that they were the reason he took as long as he did to return. I put everything, papers and money into the suitcase and put my hand on the doorknob to leave.

Daddy looked as though he was going to hug me and I wondered if I could stop him and still escape without a fuss or one big 'fair well' if I told him not to touch me. I was saved from telling him anything when he glanced down briefly at my distended belly and then sat back in his e-z boy with the remote and turned on the holovision. He acted as though I wasn't there and if he glanced after me when I closed the door behind me for the last time, I'll never know.

I had wanted to say 'goodbye' to Penny and Rhoda and her bees, but I knew better than that. I would cry and telling Rhoda anything would only get her into trouble. Much better if nobody ever heard another word from me. I carried my suitcase and walked the long walk to the compound gate. I would have to soothe myself with knowledge of her gift of honey in my suitcase and memory of her smile and Penny's nose licking my face. I would content myself with the knowlege of the miracle of a beehive and apple blossoms that set themselves.

Chapter 2: Shock

"God has mercifully ordered that the human brain works slowly; first the blow, hours afterward the bruise."

-Walter de la Mare, 'The Return'.

For the first time in my memory I slept in a strange bed that night.

It was not pleasant and I woke up with itchy welting bedbug bites and a sore throat from being so close to the waste that wasn't screened or filtered from the air here. No artificial birdsong greeted my morning, but I could hear someone hacking themselves what sounded to death next door to me. I wondered what Penny and Rhoda were doing this morning. I wondered what daddy had told Mother about where I had gone.

He would make sure that I had permission for at least forty eight hours but when I didn't show up for my hospital appointment this afternoon the timer would be ticking and my identification would have me apprehended and remanded for immediate treatment. I had to hurry.

The previous day hadn't been wasted. I had found this room to rent and I had also found a black market abortion doctor to remove 'the matter'. I had to find my way to him first thing and then I had to find the recruitment office and get off Dalton before any alert was called out on me.

The 'process' wasn't as bad as I thought it would be. I was given more fiery liquid and a sweet syrup that gave me waking nightmares while the 'doctor' worked. The dreams were dreadful and when he was finished I staggered out of his office hoping to leave the nightmares behind me. Still high on syrup and grief I found my way into the GAF recruiting office and filed my paperwork to be on the next transit out.

The Galactic Armed Forces was used to 'sudden' recruits who were eager to leave their home planets within the day and I was leaving the planet before my appointment at the hospital. I would pay to become an officer with the money in my suitcase and whatever they thought of my answers I passed the exam and was given a different uniform and badge than the first one I had rode out of Dalton on. My first night spent in a space vessel was far more pleasant then the one in the room I had rented. The bed was hard and narrow and the sheets were thin and balled with lint, but I was free. It was my own freedom that had allowed me to enlist, just like with everyone else in the GAF.

I had things I was running away from, things I didn't want to talk about and confusion that I might never figure out. The bed was free from bugs and the food was chemical but plentiful and fortified with vitamins. Best of all, I was off of Dalton and ready to see what the rest of the galaxy held... a galaxy with daddy left far behind and I would never see another sunrise framed by cooling stacks. I would see mountains and streams, real birds and even some natural bees. I would meet the love of my life and melt in his arms. I would save lives and protect people who were being victimized by people stronger than them. I was happy, I was whole and everything else I would heal.

That seemed to be true at first. The thing is, and I hope that at least a few people who read this can understand and not judge me too harshly, I was in shock.

I didn't realize how much I was hurting emotionally and physically at the first.

The day that they had taken Anastasia I had fallen into a nightmare and everything up to a certain point after that was all happening without me stopping to lick my wounds and acknowledge what I had been through. I was under attack , first from the extreme breach of my concept of reality through losing the only person who had ever really loved me, my 'Stacia, and then from Daddy.

I had run away from home, joined an intergalactic military organization where it was conceivable that I could be brutally killed in the line of duty or in the vacuum of space. I had lost my parents, my idea of safety, the sanctity of my body... I had even lost the only planet that I had ever known.

Even though I had successfully enlisted, things didn't start all at once. After I arrived at the space station I had some time to kill while the rest of my 'class' slowly trickled in. As a result, I had a bit of a lull and some time to get used to my new situation.

I signed up at GAF headquarters in Cobalt City. That was the name of the place over the wall. The subburb of Cobalt City where I had lived with my family was called the Chim Sub and I had to list my parents' address as my home address. I was pretty nervous having done that, but as it was on all my paperwork and everything there wasn't any choice. I still wasn't used to the fact that I was of a legal age and since my paperwork getting me out of Chim Sub was valid, I was accepted without any further questions asked.

Things were a little dicey for me on the medical, but since my abortion had been illegal there wasn't any sign in my forms of recent medical procedures and nobody noticed anything except some tenderness in my belly when the poked around a bit. The lady nurse asked me if that was normal for me.

I responded with, 'Well, it's normal once a month'.

She nodded and smiled at me in sympathy and a few minutes later I was given an A1 rating for officer school to follow basic training.

On Dalton, the basic training is accomplished on the orbiting space station, "Martial 43". There are several space stations around Dalton, but this one is a hundred percent owned by the GAF as are all of the Martial series. There are a lot more than forty three of them around a lot more than forty three planets. The galaxy needs a lot of protecting.

Martial 43 was very large. It was set up to be a home away from home for a lot of experts and skilled workers who were required to maintain or troubleshoot for a big Nuclear Industrial planet like Dalton. The GAF was one of the biggest investors in Dalton, as the ores were valuable as a military asset and so was the energy produced by the enormous nuclear plants. These experts were also well educated and aware of the research that showed what prolonged exposure to the air and water on Dalton could result in for their health and their chances for normal children. The only way to get people like that to come to Dalton was by giving them a space station.

Martial 43 was a GAF Training and Recreation Station. It was abbreviated to TRS but people usually called them 'Terse' for an even shorter abbreviation. As in, 'you sound a little terse today, what's up with that?'

There were all sorts of facilities on board, but my favorite thing to do was to look out the window. They were actually called 'observation ports' and they were quite large, although some of them were virtual displays and not actually on the exterior of the ship. It was extremely hard to tell the difference. After some experimentation, I discovered that the biggest difference between the two was that the exterior ports were a little bit chill if you put your fingers on it and the virtual ones were ambient in temperature.

Orbiting Dalton gave me deep thoughts about the world I had been born into and suddenly my whole life was put into perspective. Dalton was a larger-than-earth planet. It was quite large and visibly polluted from my vantage point. The atmosphere around it was a dirty red and the oceans were brown and green. In places the ocean was red. There were few lakes and rivers, what ones there were were largely tailings ponds for the many mining concerns and sluices for the same or for cooling ponds.

There were some green spaces but a lot of them had a strange red tinge to them as well. There were sprawling cities that I knew were more like ghettos, and there were the endless grids of sub divisions like Chim that radiated out from the nuclear power plants that were visible from space.

There were mines. The mines were enormous. The machines that were excavating them were giants. Even the smelters and other facilities looked like dinosaurs eating the landscape. This was the purpose of Dalton. It was the only reason I had been born there, so that I could grow up and be part of the machinery of its destruction.

Dalton was largely uninhabited before the colonists came. The atmosphere was too sparse to have organisms as complicated as say, fruit trees or cats or whales on it before Wrought Industries had terraformed it enough so that it could support human life and human industry. It had in essence been a desert planet. Some insects, some lizards and some stuff in the ocean. Algae... not a lot else. The oceans had been shallow and dirty to begin with and there was entire continent in the South that was a completely unstable volcanic mess. Dalton would never have won any beauty prizes... but what I saw beneath me had been turned into a nightmare planet.

GAF aside, my destiny had been to be born here, breed if I was at all viable after what I had been born into and then work and die here. If I was able to breed, it would be likely that my children would not be normal physically or mentally, and even less likely that their children would breed.

As I sat in the quiet observation ports and stared down at Dalton, I began to really really wonder what the point of life was.

It was on one of these depressing aerial 'tours' of Dalton that I felt the first pains.

I hadn't had my period since I had had the procedure

and at first I thought it was that sort of cramp. Then it came on again and it didn't stop. It felt like I was being squeezed and the monster that had a hold of me wouldn't let me go. My eyes went wide and my hand fluttered out to clutch the observation port. It was cold to my finger tips that scrabbled against it without gaining purchase. I was surprised it was one of the real ports and oddly soothed by it. A shard of reality amidst the knifing pain was better than what came next: dizziness and then blood, warm, trickling and humiliating down my leg.

Then blackness.

I woke up in the infirmary. I didn't remember how I had got there but my clothes had been removed and I was in a cool, clean bed.

I opened my eyes and the lights seemed crisp after the oozing, fevered darkness that I had left behind. I didn't feel great and there was a bag of Brahmlie blood substitute tapped into my arm and a couple of other tubes going into my forearm that I wobbled a bit to see if they were connected to me. I felt briefly like I was going to be sick and black out again. It was the way they made my flesh move around them, it looked like a badness.

I tried to sit up and then I lay back down again. It was much too soon.

There were other beds around me. A man was sleeping

two beds away from me and the rest were tidily made and empty. The room was obviously monitored and a smiling nurse came in a few minutes later.

"Good morning, Sasha. How are we feeling today?"

"Queasy."

I smiled nervously at the nurse who smiled back at me with bland professionalism. I wondered if they knew what had caused the bleeding, it could only have been one thing...

"You'll need to rest for a few days. You lost quite a bit of blood but Dr. Johnson fixed you up."

"I'm going to be OK?"

"I'll let you talk to the Doctor to go over the details, but yes, you'll be just fine. You need to rest and the sooner you feel like eating, the sooner you'll be on the mend."

She sat me up like I was a doll and fluffed my pillow. She raised the head of the bed so it was sitting up more. A table was raised up and produced a single of Wrought Apple juice from her pocket and a little straw. She poked the straw through the cover and handed it to me. I was drinking it before I was really aware of what had happened and she poured me a glass of water.

"There, feeling a bit better, then?"

I nodded. The queasiness had started to fade for the apple juice and for not poking the tubes coming out of me.

"Do you think you could eat some pudding? Sometimes it helps to start with sweet things. Pudding and a little piece of toast?"

"That sounds good, I think I could eat that."

She beamed at me and left the room. I was relieved that she didn't have all that in her nurse's pockets as well. It helped to convince me that I had actually woke up.

I ate the pudding and toast that the nurse brought back. She introduced herself as Sarah and reiterated her advice that I should rest. I wondered what else I could possibly do and then she showed me how to operate the holovision that was built into the table where my water and food had been set.

I turned it on and watched Verily Wrought answer questions on a morning talk show that originated from

Bradenburg. He was charming and glib, he folded his long legs and blushed when his sexual exploits were brought up and then answered with utterly charming candidness that made my own cheeks blush. The holo talk shows loved to display the nude pictures that had been bought from various hotel surveillance cameras. It was clearly a violation for the hotels to sell them, but who could really judge them when one heard how much money they had sold them for? Verily seemed to have accepted the fact that naked photos of him would happen and he dealt with it with an aplomb that was commendable.

I woke up to see Dr. Johnson's transparent grin over my bed.

I say transparent in the literal sense. I had to withhold a scream of surprise at my first sight of an actual Jellyman. I held in my exclamation, but I wasn't able to hide the look of shock and, I confess, disgust on my face.

Dalton was remarkably uniform in its inhabitants, namely, they were all human. This was for a lot of reasons, one of them being that it's a lot harder to convince most alien races that selling out your genetics and your health for a career on a nuclear mining planet is a good idea. That, and I believe some security concerns, were the biggest reasons. I think they were just all too smart to go to a place like Dalton. When you realize how many perfectly wonderful planets there are throughout the GAGA you realize how dense you would really have to be to end up on a resource world.

I was alarmed by Dr. Johnson because to someone who has never seen a Jellyman, their appearance seems quite disturbing. Jellymen are nearly entirely transparent except for their bones and their internal organs. Most blood vessels are opaque, especially the veins. Their veins and their natural pale blue color make them appear fairly blue all over and like something that incongruously might be good to snack on, some sort of candy or jello maybe.

I could see his eyes move and the movements in his tongue as he reacted to my surprise. I could tell from his heart movement alone that my reaction was terribly surprising or offensive to him. He turned off the holovision and smiled at me again.

"I'm sorry, I didn't mean to be rude."

"I know. Most natives to Dalton have never seen a Jellyman before."

He looked at my chart on his Personal Device. I got the distinct impression that he was inspecting it to give me a chance to recover rather than for any need to check out how I was doing. There were only two patients in here after all. He pulled up a chair and sat beside my bed.

"How are you feeling now, Sasha?"

I paused before answering. There was something about him that made me want to give him a real answer, not just tell him I was 'fine' and try to get rid of him as I would normally do when faced with a confrontation. I took a breath and felt my body.

"I think I'm Ok, but I feel funny somehow."

He nodded. "I had to do some surgery, you had a wound in your uterus and I had to cauterize it. Do you understand what I'm saying to you?"

I bit my lip and nodded. I didn't want to talk about what would come next. He continued.

"There is no sign of any reason why you would have had such a bleed in your official medical file, but there is an official file that was nearly lost of an ultrasound that you had on Dalton."

He paused, perfectly still except for the pulsing of his veins.

"I understand you had good reason to want to terminate the pregnancy, I'm just not sure why you went through illegal channels to do so. Were you worried that they would make you keep it?"

I felt tears start to seep out from my eyelids. I squeezed them shut and shook my head and then changed it into a nod. "I didn't really... but I was worried... I was upset and I didn't really know what I was doing."

He was still sitting calmly. He seemed oblivious to my upset. I watched his heart bumping in his chest and the thumping rhythm of the blood moving under his clear skin. I felt my own heart calming in response. He smiled, so gently at me I broke into tears. He put a hand on my shoulder, through my gown it felt cool and soft, as gentle as his smile.

"It's alright, Sasha. You aren't going to be in trouble and the important thing now is that you're safe. Do you understand that, that you're safe?"

I nodded at him again. "Am I going to get kicked out of the GAF?"

He shook his head. "No, it's certainly not the worst thing that someone enlisted in the GAF has ever done. It's mostly something that is going to affect your strength and stamina in early training."

"Will it affect my bid to become an officer?"

"No, it's irrelevant to most of your life now... but Sasha, I want you to know that whatever reason underneath that you didn't want to do things through legal channels, these things can come back and affect you. You need to keep on top of your mental situation in a case like this because having something like this hiding in your mind could affect your future in the GAF."

"You mean I might be crazy?"

"No, I'm saying... I'm saying that I know you don't want to talk right now, but that you might need to later on. If you need to, I'm telling you as friend that you have to follow up on that need."

His earnest intensity made me agree. He patted my shoulder with his strange cool, hand once more and checked on the man who was still sleeping two beds down from me.

I was exhausted and relieved that I didn't need to talk about what had happened anymore. I watched some more holovision with Verily Wrought on it and fell asleep again.

I had to stay in the infirmary for several days while they kept an eye on me to make sure that nothing else opened up. I didn't dare ask anyone if I had wrecked myself so that I could never try to have a baby again. I didn't want to know and it would have been too much to find out I couldn't. Being able to have babies on Dalton was such a gift. If it was gone, it would be one more thing to hate Daddy for and I didn't think I could handle that sort of rage.

I imagined smashing an observation port and falling through the atmosphere in my anger and need to get to him and kill him for taking away my ability to ever become a mother. I fell asleep and dreamt I was holding Anastasia when she was a baby and her hair had that special smell only an infant has.

I woke up and the infirmary was mildly in chaos.

The man who had been asleep had left or been moved and they were rushing in people on stretchers. Sarah closed the privacy screen around my bed with the push of a button and it dampened the sound but I was feeling better and my curiousity roused me.

I had to drag a cart with me to bring my bag of blood (It had been changed while I slept and a fresh plump bag dangled from it now) and the other mysterious tubes that went into a little cabinet where a machine quietly made a 'whirrrrr' noise. Dr. Johnson was attaching a device to a man and packing his chest area with bandages that filled to cover the areas of his torso that were covered in burns.

The Jellyman saw me standing and watching and

gestured at me impatiently. "See those red and grey packs? Grab four or five of them for me?"

I nodded, Sarah spared me a glance and saw that I was under Dr. Johnson's orders now ignored me and went back to working with tight efficiency on a woman who appeared to have been burned on her hands. I grabbed him the packs and wheeled my set up over to him. He ripped them open and bits of things fell out of them that looked like string. They wriggled like living things and started moving to the charred skin. It looked exactly like they were eating the burnt flesh.

He checked the man's vital signs and nodded. His heartbeat was rapid. My own heartbeat seemed to race to match his. He moved to the woman who Sarah had been tending.

"Sarah, did you page Dr. Thumbert?"

"I did..."

"Where the hell is he? And where is Richa?"

"She's gone to find Dr. Thumbert."

"Where is everyone else?" His voice was growling. "Sarah, go see who else you can find. There could be more people coming in still, I heard as many as a dozen. We're going to need more help."

He gestured for me to follow him. I grabbed more of the red and grey packets. Those things were pretty neat.

I helped him with the gel packs that were actually nanobots that worked as a false skin to protect the burned areas from infection. The strings were genetically enhanced and enlarged bacterium that ate only the charred flesh that would otherwise need to be cut of in surgery. They fell to the floor after they had done their business and then I swept them up and put them into the incinerator.

The other doctor and two more nurses came in as I was finishing and I felt dizzy again. Dr. Johnson gestured towards my bed, I took off towards it and my privacy screen. Probably it wasn't procedure to get the girl with the botched abortion and a bag of blood to help out with burn victims; it didn't seem very hygenic somehow.

There had been a shuttle accident and some of the accident victims had been my new classmates. There weren't any fatalities, but some of the people needed longer to heal. Since the group that had enlisted was quite small so far it was decided from on high that general training would be put off for an extra month while some of my class, and of course myself as well, had a chance to heal.

Dr. Johnson examined me the next day and then intsructed Sarah to remove the tubes from me. I looked away while Sarah removed them and Dr. Johnson hummed and read over files on his PD. Sarah left and Dr. Johnson pulled his chair over close to the bed.

"I wanted to thank you for helping out yesterday. It's likely you saved some people from some scarring, infection, or even worse. It was quick thinking and you helped even though you weren't in a good way yourself."

I mumbled an embarrassed, 'Of course...'

"It wasn't something that everyone could have done, or would have thought to do. I wanted to ask you a big favor, because that's what happens when you do something right in life, people want you to do it again and do it more."

I looked at him. My eyes were somber and large.

"I want to ask the GAF if I can train you. I know there are provisions for it, it just doesn't happen all the time. I think you're a natural healer, Sasha. It's a great thing to have on your GAF

67

resume as well. It will put you in line for promotions not available to people without first aid field training."

I was already nodding my head in consent though he continued to outline the advantages to me. I wanted to learn more very badly.

Chapter 3: Interlude and Denial

"You can't get away from yourself by moving from one place to another"

-Ernest Hemingway, "The Sun Also Rises"

I slept in the infirmary another night and after that I was moved back to the quarters where I would be spending the rest of training. Most of the beds were full now, but the one I had already chosen and had my things on before I ended up in the infirmary had been left undisturbed.

My roommates and I were all a little standoffish. It was like we were all pretending that the others were figments of their imagination. I was good with this approach and I started training in the infirmary every day while the others hung out in the gym or in the entertainment and holovision room.

Dr. Johnson was wonderful as a teacher. He seemed to have an intuition for when I was around and available to take part in a new procedure. He could sense when I was ready for a new piece of learning and I didn't feel pushed at all. He was uncanny how he could predict me.

I also had a sense with him that I knew him somehow. We could sit and be quiet together and it didn't seem awkward.

It was Sarah that started to give me problems.

I had been born into my neighbourhood in Dalton and I had never had to be the 'new girl' before. I hadn't actually been cognizant of this as a potential problem. Our school in Dalton had been practically solid at the seams and we didn't see much new traffic in it. It didn't occur to me that people would be territorial of their domain and protect it from intruders, and besides, I had liked Sarah and had thought that naturally she would like me in return.

While she was my nurse she had been so professional and kind with me. I was surprised when I came in in my GAF uniform pants and a black t-shirt that marked me as a 'not patient' and her entire demeanor towards me changed.

All she said was, "Oh, helping out, are we?" before turning on her heel and leaving with her cup of kaffe. It was weird. Dr. Johnson came in right after her and she smiled at him and then spared and extra glare over her shoulder for me. I realized that was not a good sign but Dr. Johnson seemed oblivious towards the sudden tension and told me to call him Stephen which was the closest english name to the nearly unpronounceable syllables of his Jellic name..

He offered me a cup of kaffe and then we started going through the extensive paperwork necessary to get me through the back door into the infirmary to get my paramedic training.

Stephen left several times to go and check on patients and do other doctor things and each time he left, it seemed like Sarah had some reason to come in and check on me. I was more and more convinced that she was 'checking up' on me rather than checking on me as the day went by. I had never been very worldly of the machinations of women but even I began to have some suspicions of what I had walked into.

Dr. Johnson seemed to understand on some level that there was a conflict going on and would smile mirthlessly at Sarah's jibes of me and if she stepped out of line while he was in the room he would mock her about it until Sarah found a reason to leave. After that he would laugh with me about something, not about Sarah, but something else. Sarah didn't know we werent' laughing about her, but I'm sure she heard our laughter from the other room and this embarrassed me.

I felt even worse when I saw her wipe an angry tear from the side of her face one day and I realized that I was being mean even if I wasn't actually saying anything. I watched Dr. Johnson after this for awhile, trying to understand why he was being so kind to me and yet so casually cruel to any consideration about Sarah.

I couldnt' see why he was singling her out. She was competent at her job, she was good with the patients and she was intuitive about figuring out what Dr. Johnson needed next and where he would be at any given time in the space station. It was one particular moment where I finally figured out an aspect of what was going on.

Dr. Johnson was turning from a tray of gauze and I was learning how to sew up a small wound and how to treat it so that they wouldn't have any pain when I did the stitches. The patient was the pilot from a private ship and he had agreed to use old fashioned needle and thread stitches in the spirit of learning and as he said, 'getting a wicked scar to impress the ladies'.

It wasn't going to be that wicked, it was only about two and half inches on his forearm. I was working on the stiches and as the doctor turned back towards me, Sarah somehow managed to run right into him and spilt the tray of gauze and needles and iodine everywhere. She rarely ever mistepped like that and she blushed a furious scarlet and Dr. Johnson cursed roundly at her clumsiness. She ran out of the room without trying to help, my patient and I both saw the tears that were streaming down her red face and our eyebrows raised. Somehow, this finally made it clear to me that Sarah had a crush on the doctor.

I finished sewing up the patient and decided that it was best not to talk to Sarah. She seemed so embarrassed and I knew that in that sort of situation I wouldn't want to have someone talk to me. Then something else started to become clear to me... maybe Dr. Johnson sort of liked me.

At first it was just noticing that when I asked a question he would answer, sounding happy and excited to share his information with me, and then I noticed that he treated Sarah as though she was stupid if she asked an equally legitimate question. I overheard Ange, one of the other nurses teasing Sarah.

It was just one comment about how Stephen had found fresh meat to go after and then I realized that the 'meat' they were talking about was me. I put togther that he laughed at my jokes, which historically only Anastasia had ever laughed at, and he would linger anytime we touched... our fingers, our hips as we moved around the lab or the examination room...

With my heart racing I tried to analyze my own feelings about Stephen Johnson. I had never thought of him, not that way. I liked him a lot but to be perfectly honest, I found him to be very alien. Being able to see his bones and his blood vessels, even to see the outside of his brain as he analyzed and thought... it was alien and alien wasn't attractive.

But it was flattering. He was very intelligent and he was so very kind... well, to everyone except Sarah. I wondered what she had done to him break his heart and make him so angry. I automatically placed the blame for the failure of the relationship on Sarah. How could Dr. Johnson go from being so kind to so callous unless she had done something... in a totally groundless leap of logic I decided that she had had an affair on him and only realized her mistake after breaking his heart. That was a fanciful and absurd assumption and it turned out that I had it all exactly wrong.

I went to the store and used a few of my hoarded credits to buy some lipstick and eyeliner. I wore them into the lab the next day and noticed that there was a tingle when our fingers touched. I let our fingers touch for that extra moment and watched the transluscent corners of his mouth quirk up into a smile. My fingers started to shake and I felt... excited. My breath caught and I liked the feeling I had of being out of control. I liked the sudden flush of heat across my abdomen, I liked the shaking of my hands, I liked the ragged edge to my breath. I moved my hair behind my ear and waited to see what he would do, to see where he would go next. He moved away from me and I felt a surge of disappointment and then I heard the sound of footsteps.

"Dr. Johnson, there's a patient to see you... he said he had a head injury but he walked in here without any problems... should I get him to lie down?"

Dr. Johnson cursed in Jellyman under his breath and moved Sarah aside to go out to tend the patient. She looked at me and her eyes narrowed perceptibly. I watched her, trying to keep my face vague but knowing that a horribly blush was spreading up my neck and across my cheeks. She shook her head at me and turned on her heel to follow Johnson to tend the patient. It was no good, she and I both knew it but she seemed to have an odd insistence in folllowing things with Stephen through to their embarrassing conclusions. She came back into the lab, her voice was filled with cold rage and she didn't bother to conceal the glare in her eyes in the slightest.

"The Doctor would like your assistance with the patient... Sasha." She managed to turn my name into a threat.

She seemed to know that I understood now where things stood in the office and all attempts at trying to suppress her anger with me had vanished. She blocked the door so I had to turn sideways to get past her to do as Dr. Johnson had asked.

Dr. Johnson had the young cadet laid out on a flat board and he showed me how to hold the injured neck in place so that nothing new would happen to hurt the patient more. He had shown me how to do it before using myself or Sarah or Ange as the patient but it felt different doing it with somone who was actually injured. He felt like jagged bits of glass were stuck in his neck when I touched it with my hands. There wasn't anything physical like that, it was just a sense and when I moved him the slightest bit out of the optimum way I imagined that it was like rolling it around in glass and had to work not to flinch from him. Once he was strapped down we were able to lift him up and move him to the scanner.

Afterwards, I was asked to lunch with Dr. Johnson. I blushed again... hard. I wondered what it would be like to never blush and watched his food get chewed through his clear cheek and then get swallowed until it disappeared beneath the collar of his shirt. He covered the side of his face with his napkin selfconsiously. I looked down at my chicken salad sandwhich, I was embarrased that I had embarrased him.

He cleared his throat. "I was wondering if you wanted to watch the Holo with me tonight. There is a movie..."

"Yes." I blurted out without even letting him finish.

"That would be nice... It would be nice to get to know you better, Sasha."

We finished our lunch in near silence. I had to work very hard not to be clumsy when we returned to organizing the lab. He kept brushing up against me, leaning over me to reach something. He was much taller than me and when I looked up I would see the blood vessels in a transluscent wrist wrapped around bone sticking out of his lab coat and watch his pulse as his finger bones grabbed the big jugs on the shelves over me. He smelled warm and a little like something that I couldn't identify at the time but I later on realized was the ocean.

I bought contraceptives from the store and then I looked

on my PD only to realize that Jellymen were a different species and there had never been a successful breeding between a human and a Jellyman. Then I wondered what was wrong with me that I thought that making babies with someone I had only called by his first name over chicken salad a few hours ago was even an option... or rather, trying to not make babies with him... you know what I mean.

Then I decided that I didn't care and I brought them with me anyhow. I also bought eye shadow and mascara and lifted my chin defiantly to the girl who rang me through, daring her in my mind to ask me about my evening's plans.

He let me into his room and it was much more normal than I had been afraid it would be. I had been worried that it would be a big deal and that he would have dimmed the lights and put on romantic music. I worried that the whole thing would be like a bad Holo that my mother would watch and cry over.

It was brightly lit and there were stacks of journals all over the place. He had several cats that climbed on everything and made me sneeze until he matter of factly reached into a kitchen drawer and took out a hypo and injected me with antihistimines.

"I'm sorry about the cats, it seems like everyone from Dalton has allergies so I keep hypos in here now for any company that I might have."

I squinched my eyes shut and nodded, hoping it would kick in soon. I tried to wipe my eyes with a kleenix so that I didn't smear my new mascara all over my cheeks. When I went to the bathroom I discovered that it hadn't worked as well as I had hoped and went about wiping off my raccoon eyes and trying to repair the damage to my red, swollen with plenty of cold water. I wouldn't say that I looked *sexy* when I was done but I looked a little less horrible at least.

Stephen was banging pots around in the kitchen and his cats were wandering around on the counters and winding around his legs. I was very upset that my first time seeing cats for real was going so badly. I had never had a hard time with allergies around Penny but this was completely different. These animals were so soft.

I reached down and petted one who seemed to have decided that she should groom any extra fur off on my pants. She was blackish brown with streaks of orange. Her eyes were bright green all over with no whites at all and a little slit where her pupil should be. She looked up at me and I had the distinct impression that she was laughing at me.

"They look like they should be able to talk." I was surprised that I had spoken my thought out loud and smiled shyly at Stephen.

"Not these ones... I think I'd go mad if they could talk, look how demanding they are even without the ability of speech. I'd feel like a slave in my own house."

The at I had been petting mewled plaintively at me and I realized he was right, but I hadn't realized that any cats could talk. "Are these ones... umm, not as smart as the ones who talk?"

"It depends, they are genetically engineered from regular cats. These ones are just cats, from earth, but very exotic for me. There aren't a lot of furry things on my home planet. "

"Do dogs ever talk?"

"Well, I'm no expert on them, but I have heard that some have been enhanced to do so. You can genetically modify nearly anything to talk if you have money and the will to do it. It's mostly a question of why you would in most cases."

"Loneliness," I blurted.

"Definitely loneliness," He agreed.

"I think if I was going to get a talking animal, it would be a dog."

"You don't like my cats?"

"Dogs don't make me sneeze," I answered evasively. The cats were unnerving to me in a way that Penny had never been. If Penny could talk I thought she'd be the best friend ever, well, nearly the best friend ever, I ammended.

"There is an entire planet of Dog people, the Canines," Stephen remarked as he cooked. "I know that they held some protests about having widespread genetically modified talking dogs. I guess I can't blame them for being upset."

I didn't understand why they would be upset but nodded agreeably. There was so much about the universe that I didn't know. Growing up on a remote resource planet had left me extremely sheltered from most of the galaxy and I had come to understand I was a complete hick. I knew nothing about the different races of people out in the galaxy. Jellyman Stephen was my first encounter with an alien, although technically I guess Penny kind of counted as an alien being as well.

It seemed as though I had also been invited for dinner as

a guest only, so I amused myself by snooping around his apartment while we chatted. He didn't seem to mind and I was curious about him. Stephen Johnson had a lot of plants as well as papers and cats. The cats seemed to come out of everywhere, I counted seven by the end of the evening but I had the unsettling suspicion that there were more that I had missed somehow. The room was cool but humid and there were vents that occassionally sprayed out a chill mist into the room. I wasn't exactly cold but I felt like I could shortly be quite cold if the mist kept spraying.

I thought about what it would be like if I married Dr. Johnson. They were idle little fantasies but I found it hard to imagine living in this apartment in the chill damp air that seemed to be always circulating and blowing with his seven cats and constant injections for my allergies. It was such a mess, of course we would have to find a way to organize all the papers and get shelves for the plants...

What was I even thinking? Imagination-stop it.

He made spaghetti with meatballs for us and afterwards we sat on his couch, surrounded by cats and watched, "Death Be Not Around" with James Haskins in it. He took me in his arms when we moved into the living room and pulled me towards him as though we had always cuddled up on the couch. I felt his warmth, so much warmer than the room and closed my eyes so I could only just see the Holo through my eyelashes.

"Are you cold?"

"A little," I said. In all honesty I was trying to keep my teeth from chattering, I had gotten very cold after we ate. He was a good cook and a lot of his food was fresh, some of it from the plants in this very room, others imported, a few of the things he had I suspected were off the black market but I knew I wasn't galactic enough to know for sure.

He pulled a blanket overtop of us and I worried about the cat hair on it bringing on another allergic attack but at least for the moment I was fine. He put his arms around me and I burrowed in, both for the warmth and for the opportunity to be close to another human being and also because he smelled like the ocean.

His hand trailed from my shoulder to the edge of my breast. He had large hands, larger than most human men have. In all he was the size of a very large human but because he was all clear around the edges it was easy to think he was a more regular size. His fingers traced circles on the edges of my breasts and I wanted him to do more to me. I made no effort to move away, I opened myself up to more. We didn't see much of the movie, or at least, I didn't. I was waiting every moment to wonder what he might touch next, how far he might go. It was only at the part where Sally realizes that her uncle has become Death that he lifted up the edge of my t-shirt and touched my bare skin.

I moaned softly and bit my lip. He looked down at me with kindly smiling eyes that would never blink and started to explore me in earnest. I wriggled and sighed under his touch and when he undid my pants I helped to get them off of my hips and when he stood up and started to remove his own clothes I wondered what a transluscent man would look like once the pants came off and helped him with his fly.

I fell asleep in his arms, my curiosity on the matter and some other matters as well thoroughly sated. It wasn't until I woke up, sticky with a strange warmish that I realized that a Jellyman bed was more jelly than bed.

Chapter 4: The Love of a Jellyman

"In very different ways, the possibility that the universe is teeming with life, and the opposite possibility that we are totally alone, are equally exciting. Either way, the urge to know more about the universe seems to me irresistible, and I cannot imagine that anybody of truly poetic sensibility could disagree."

-Richard Dawkins

Waking up in a bed that covers you in chill pink slime after a night of intense love making was an uniquely disturbing experience. Stephen was still asleep and I woke up with his arm draped over me, entangled and naked in his pumping blood vessels and bones. I moved his arm and he rolled over away from me, clutching his pillow and smiling. The bed was gooshy like it was filled with water but it was also a little bit warm and it was pink and the pink had transferred itself to me in the night. How had I not noticed the bed when we had come to it?

I thought about the previous night, it had started on the couch and we had taken off each other's clothes. He was an intimidating presence naked. His heart was pounding and with each flush of the muscle it made his chest seem to glow with redness. I had been with only two men in my life and even though the second one I had been with had been pretty rushed and it had been dark, I was absolutely sure that It hadn't moved around all on Its own and I was also sure that It hadn't nestled in a cluster of tinier moving, wriggling penis-like organs. His spaghetti was partially digested and stained his stomach and intestines. I looked away, embarrased that I was staring at him once more. I wondered what he thought of my opaque body, so much less interesting than his own. I wondered if it was weird for him too.

He lifted my chin to meet his eyes. "It's all right for you to look, Sasha. I want you to be comfortable, I want you to enjoy me."

Then I looked at him in earnest, as I had wanted to do all along. Except for being a little large and for the mass of moving organs in his groin, he was very much similar to the other men. There were a couple of internal organs I knew from the lessons he had taught me that humans didn't have but they weren't very noticeable. I wouldn't have known that they didn't belong if he hadn't been teaching me about anatomy to further my understanding of medicine and emergency field surgery.

He ran his fingers through my hair and traced the outline of my jaw with his soft yet firm jelly finger. I put my hand on his chest and I could feel his heartbeat stronger than I could feel my own heart beat in my own chest. It seemed to resonate and impact things more than human flesh and when it throbbed I felt more of my self-control yield to him. I could feel his member moving against me, it seemed to be seeking entry without any assistance from Stephen and I had a moment of revulsion and tried to pull away. Stephen hushed me, he hummed and the vibration from his humming made me forget what had been upsetting me.

He had hummed frequently throughout the sex and what had first felt alien and upsetting turned to feeling erotic and pleasing. I submitted to him after that without question and even when he pushed my head down to the writhing transluscent mass I took it in eagerly. I wanted him and the humming to never stop.

Excerpt from Encyclopaedia Galactica:

"Jellicmin, commonly called 'Jellymen' are native to the planet Jellic in the Alpha Quadrant. They had limited space travel before being encountered by the GAGA but were an enthusiastic and open member to GAGA affiliation. They soon gained access to GAGA space routes in exchange for the resources that the Jellicmin had to offer.

The Jellymen are unusual in that all of their muscles, tendons and ligaments are nearly completely transluscent. They are solid but considerably more pliant than the average human is accustomed to feeling flesh. Their blood gives them most of their visibility and their food is highly visible when being absorbed and digested as well. They are at home in a moist, cool environment and enjoy beds that have been designed to provide a viscous emolient while they sleep. These beds are often called 'clam shells' and are often designed to mimic the shape of clams as well, although that is inconsequential to their purpose.

Jellymen are intelligent and practical and share many common traits with humans that have made them integrate especially well into the human regions of the GAGA.

They are not able to interbreed with humans or most other alien life forms but they have made several 'mules' with dolphins and other cetaceans. They excrete a sound that has been inaccurately compared to the purring of a cat that they use for soothing and anethetizing friends or foes. They are extremely soothing when they choose to be and can hypnotize with the beat of their pulse and the vibrations that they put out. They also excrete a substance when sexually aroused that can cause further pliancy and has been shown to have highly addictive qualities, especially in humans."

I read the article the next morning while I was mooning around the lab, trying to learn how to test for a new form of influenza that was storming through the Delta sector. It wasn't hard stuff, but my mind was elsewhere. I was worried about what the article said about the possibility of addiction because I was feeling a need to be back in Stephen's arms that I had never felt before.

Sarah seemed to be fully aware of what had transpired between Dr. Johnson and me the night before. She was ignoring me and walked away from me when I asked her to hand me a stethoscope even though it was right in front of a patient. She was even somewhat rude to Stephen and usually he was immune to any of her bad moods. She didn't have a nice word for anyone that day and I pitied the patients she had to examine and the rough hands she used.

It was nearly the end of my free time before basic training and I realized that it was going to be strange to not spend every single day in the infirmary. I fretted about being away from Stephen. It was irrational since I had signed up to be an officer so I would be shipped off to the Officer Training Planet, nicknamed Easty-Westy, in no time. My connection to Stephen was beyond tenuous. In fact, in the lab, he was much more calm and far less attentive to me than he had been the day before.

I was concerned about the sudden shift in attention away from me until we were nearly at the end of the day and then he asked me if I wanted to come back to his room again. I nodded, noting out of the corner of my eye that Sarah had overheard our exchange. That night went much the same as the night before. We had dinner which he cooked and then we watched a holo together until it devolved into sex.

I was feeling wonderful the next morning and I had never seen myself have such pink colouring. My eyes were large and shining. My hair was glossy and had a wildness to it that made me tie it back into a ponytail with extra effort to keep the strands from unwinding themselves around my face. It was like my body was hyper-charged with energy. My mind, however, was hyper-worried about the mention of addiction and the feeling that I had that my senses had been messed with. I reluctantly decided that I had to break up with Stephen and 'come down' off of what I was quite certain was a Jellyman addiction.

I had heard that I wass going to have to start basic training in the next couple of weeks. They were trying to find out when our sergeant would be shipped in but he was the last person for which we were waiting. Stephen was spending a lot of time running various field drills with me and he said that I was ready to be certified as a field doctor.

His sudden proclamation startled and embarrased me and derailed me from my firm plan to tell him that our time together had been fun but that I wasn't interested in having a relationship and that I had to focus on basic training now.

Originally I was going to get my field medic certication. That alone was generally a pricey process but Stephen had filled out all the paperwork and written letters for me and had managed to find me a scholarship to get the field medic paperwork filed. That had been going above and beyond in my opinion. Filing for me to become a field doctor was a much, much more intense and above all, expensive procedure. As

89

soon as he brought out the idea, I wanted it very badly and I knew that there was a chance he might keep on with it, but then again, he might not.

It wasn't as though I was breaking up with him for any real reason, assuming we were actually, 'going out' and he didn't just consider it a casual thing. I wanted to see more of him, I craved him... and that made me worry that the article in the Encyclopedia Galactica wasn't fooling about addictive properties. With that sort of power, he could essentially turn Sarah, or myself, into his willing slave if he wanted to.

I had no idea that he intended to make me a field doctor. I was stunned. He asked if I wanted to come over for supper again and I said yes.

I was starting to feel at home in his cluttered quarters and my allergies were getting better from the inocculation against the allergens that Stephen had given me the day before. He said it could take as long as a month before I would be really comfortable around that cats but that I could pick them up, pet them or even sleep with them once the anti-allergen shot reached its full effect.

"I thought a celebration was in order."

He pulled out a dark, tall necked bottle and started fiddling with the cork on it. "You're going to be a doctor."

"I feel badly about you paying for it," I said the words and they were truth, but I wanted it so badly that I didn't really mean them beyond a pleasantry. If he decided to tell me that he wouldnt' pay for it, I thought I would beg him to reconsider.

He shrugged. "It's no problem for me, and it will help you out in your career beyond what you could know right now. It is likely to save your life on multiple occassions. Unlike even medics, they don't tend to throw doctors in with the rest of the cannon fodder."

"It's a lot of money..."

"You're a nice girl, Sasha. I like to see good things happen to nice people sometimes. Just think of me as a kind Uncle or the father you never had."

After he said that, having sex was decidely more odd to me. The tentacles in a family context made it seem all the more peculiar. The next morning I woke up once more before the doctor and went and had a shower to get the clam shell slime off of me from his bed.

We spent all day running drills and I went home with him that evening but we didn't have sex this time. He helped me study for the doctor's exam and encouraged me. In between practicing procedures on real patients and pretending to do them on Sarah (who was a remarkably good sport once we got going), I tried to think my way through the quagmire that was my relationship with Stephen Johnson.

I liked him, but I didn't want to spend my life with him and I didn't think that he wanted to spend his life with me, or probably any human. He was more closely related to dolphins and whales than he was to me. He had paid the licensing and testing fees, now all that was left was to take the test and be certified by a third party. We went through everything until I thought my brain was going to leak out my ears and then he would rub my shoulder and my head and we would end up back in the clamshell bed, rolling over each other and wake up exhausted the next morning.

I was able to be tested in only a couple more days and I decided to take the evening off from studying and see if it helped to clear my head. We were eating dinner. He had made some sort of meatloaf that was delicious. I wanted to talk to him, but I didn't know where to start. He started for me.

"Are you nervous about starting basic training?"

"I'm feeling all sorts of ways... I'm mostly nervous about the test though."

"Don't be nervous about the test. Try to be philisophical about it, if you pass it, it's a bonus that you never expected. If you don't pass, you will still get credited as a field medic and that's a bonus as well. But, Sasha, I do think you will pass. You have a natural feel for medicine and you have been retaining all the information, you will do fine."

"Except for this morning when I thought the liver was on the wrong side of that patient."

"I blame myself for that, you see my liver all the time and it's on the wrong side for a human."

"I need to tell you that I don't love you," I blurted out.

"Why would you say that?"

"Because you've done so much for me and I've done nothing for you and I meant to stop seeing you before you told me about becoming a field doctor."

Sometimes my mouth gets set to 'nervous diarrhea'.

Stephen smiled at me with that intense kindness. "I know that. It's not mentioned in most of the entries about Jellymen, but our kind is very sensitive to changes in scent. I could tell when we woke up that day you were bothered. I was glad that the qualifying papers I had sent out came that day, they were a nice distraction to you going through all the distress of breaking up with me awkwardly."

"You knew? Then why did you keep on with me?"

"Are you sure you want to know, Sasha?"

I nodded stubbornly. He looked down at the table and then folded his hands on his lap. It was an oddly prudish gesture coming from Stephen.

"Alright, Sasha, I distracted you with becoming a field doctor to avoid a breakup because I enjoy you. I especially enjoy your body although I think you are a gifted and sensitive girl. Paying for this is much cheaper than going to a vacation planet and paying for company that would be far less engaging both mentally and physically."

I felt thoroughly smacked in the face. I found I had to gasp for air and my voice was squeaky.

"You are paying for sex with me by buying training? What about that thing you said... about the uncle?"

He looked uncomfortable. "Sasha, we all say things about ourselves that we want to believe. Sometimes they are even true half the time. You're old enought not to be silly about all this, aren't you?"

I again felt choked for an answer. I had thought I was using him and now he was saying that I was a cheap hooker he had used for his own purposes and furthermore, that he assumed that of course I would be okay for it.

I thought about my dad giving me money in exchange for my silence about the baby. I looked at Stephen's kind and concerned transparent smile and I decided that I guessed this was a better deal after than I had had so far in life. I decided that I was okay with it after all.

Chapter 5: Learning Curve

"You can never take anything personally. Just a story. It's not their fault that they want to kick you and it's certainly not yours. It's just the way things are. Sometimes you need to hear the worst, so you have no fear in waht you do and learn to work around the what-have-you."

-'Initially NO', Percipience: Outside the Range of the Understood Senses.

I had abandoned my bunkmates for nearly three weeks. They had piled their bags on my bunk in retribution. I had finished my exam and I had my Field Doctor certificate. I knew that that was something that was rare and difficult and I had pride in the fact that it was my very first accomplishment as an adult I didn't know what to think about my means of getting the money for it, I decided that it didn't matter. I hadn't slept with Stephen to manipulate him, I had had a crush on him plain and simple. It was all the later bits that got tangled.

He and I were okay. He gave me a purple syrup with a wink and told me that it would help with the cravings.

I took it and he was right. I thought about him and I missed him, but it was oddly devoid of the gooey middle bits that had made me feel like the whole business was more unseemly than it actually was. I had offered to keep helping out in the office but he had told me to save that up as something different to do when I needed to get away from the endless physical training. His knowing look worried me. I decided that basic training was likely to be very much harder than I had thought.

I fell asleep that night and had the sort of dream where you know you are dreaming even while it feels exactly like the real thing.

I was lying on my bottom bunk and I opened my eyes and Anastasia was looking down at me. She was clutching her big brown teddy bear and when she saw that my eyes were open she smiled her small, mute smile, tucked a loose strand of her long dark hair behind her ear and then extended the same hand towards me.

I put my hand in hers, knowing as I did so that she wasn't really here.

She had come to me like this before, but not since she had been taken from me. There had been the odd occasion where we had slept apart, or when she had something that she had to tell me in her inner words, and those were the times that she would come to me.

We walked out of the bunk room hand in hand. Most of the room was darkened and only my bunk bed existed in that dream place. The bunk terminated in jagged spikes like a disturbing four poster bed. The only light in the room pooled in from the open doorway where Anastasia led me. The doorway didn't lead into the corridor of the space station, instead it led into a seemingly endless vista, stars were overhead, bright and untwinkling. She led me out into the open space for a time and I had a hard time finding the doorway I had come from or even the direction in which it lie. I felt anxiety rise up as it seemed to be only me and Anastasia and this blackened heaven but she wasn't afraid and her hand was soft and warm in mine and so I followed without question.

After a time she stopped and she dropped my hand and pointed at a bright shining star that nevertheless seemed somehow occluded, as though I was looking at it through a haze of blood or darkness.

"What is it, 'Stasia? What are you showing me?"

She opened and closed her hand, looking back at me as she tried to find her voice. "That's me now. That's where I am."

"They took you to that star?"

She nodded, grateful for my understanding. "But Anastasia, I don't know the name of the star... or how to find it. I don't know the stars."

"Then find it."

I nodded my own agreement after a slight pause. It was tempting to argue with her, it was tempting to point out the many obstacles in my path but if I ever wanted to see the light of my whole galaxy again, I had to just find a way to do as she said. She had travelled a great distance to give me the information she had brought to me, and the only options I had were to try or to not try.

I looked where she pointed.

I hadn't learned much about star mapping then, and it was hard to figure out what would be important. I didn't know what the stars looked like around Dalton as they were very hard to see through the atmosphere and I had had very little time since arriving to look at them from the windows of the station. I hadn't really thought to look at them to see their patterning or their location. They moved around the space station and seemed like a limitless and random array to my eyes.

The star Anastasia had pointed out to me was very bright and clear. But from my understanding, that didn't mean it was bigger or younger, it just meant that from where ever we were postitioned in this strange between place, we were a bit closer to it. If my perspective in the galaxy were different from the station orbiting Dalton, it could look very small, so the size might not be the best way to tell.

I started to look for landmarks. The star looked a little like an eye held onto the face of some sort of snout. I decided that another spattering of stars looked a little like the ear and then my brain had connected the dots and I saw that the star she had shown to me was the eye of a boar. He was bristling with stars, he was a wild boar. I saw that a man stood over him, the man was naked but fearless, he held a net of stars in one hand with which I knew he would try to confound and entangle the raging boar in, and he held a spear in the other hand. The spear was not held poised for a killing shot, but rather was slightly defensive and one of the boar's tusks was too close. I thought the man was really nothing more then a boy, a brave boy who had dared to fight a boar and now was likely in over his head. I looked at the frozen tableau for a long time, feeling as though at any minute it would begin to move and the matter would resolve for better or for worse, but of course it didn't. It had been frozen in this spot since long before my birth and would continue for a long time to come.

The stars were moving, even if the story wasn't ready to progress between boy and boar at this moment and I felt myself falling to sleep within the dream and gently collapsed at Anastasia's feet.

The dream deepened and I awoke in a strange place. I was underwater, but even so I could breathe. Tubes went down my throat and my nose was blocked. There were wires coming out of my head and chest and there were intravenous tubes coming out of both my wrists. I was floating on my back and even though I could see the tubes and feel their invasion, I felt the calmness of Anastasia on me and I knew that she had taken me to the eye of the boar. I was tagging along in her body the way I knew she often had tagged along in mine. This was where she had been put after she had been taken from her home and family so that my Daddy could get his money and he and mom could both feel safe from the boogeyman that they feared in Anastasia's powers.

I felt angry and betrayed, but Anastasia didn't.

It's so hard to see someone you love sold out, and when they don't get angry, when they just forgive, it leaves you unsure of your own feelings. Surely, the one who has been wronged has the final say on whether or not anger is permitted, but yet, if they were disabused for their kindness and forgiveness... it was too hard to think about in my dream within a dream inside my sister's body and I let the thoughts and feelings slide away. They left with little imprint, much the same way that the turmoils of the world left Anastasia largely unruffled and I let the gentle currents in the warm fluid soothe me.

Really, it wasn't so bad being here. It was boring, but it was boring for me. I wondered if Anastasia was bored and I could feel her smile and shrug. Then I saw a picture in my/our mind of a coloring book and a half colored in flower. She

101

missed coloring but otherwise she wasn't so very unhappy. We sat for awhile in the vat, just feeling the soothingness of being close mentally once more. She missed her teddy bear and she missed the way trees looked with leaves when there was wind and also when there was not wind. Most of all she missed me. I missed her most of all as well.

There was something else in her mind too. It was something that I felt she had actually brought me to see, but also something that she didn't want to show me. I pried at her secret gently, like pulling at the closed up petal wings of an apple blossom, but she pulled the secret away from me and so I let it go.

After an unknown time there was a sound as though an alert had gone off somewhere outside in the world where everything wasn't still in the womb. It was a vibration and a pitch and then doors slid open and people walked in. Anastasia wanted to close her/our eyes, but I wanted to see and so I opened them again. There were men and some women and their uniforms were green, but brighter green then I had seen in the colors of the GAGA I was familiar with . They wore arm patches that were emblazoned in bright mustard yellow, two nested chevrons, a symbol that looked like a chair with two legs, or a standing cupboard. Over top, a disembodied wing like that of a dove's wing or perhaps it was more like a stylized eagle's wing was emblazoned.

One of the badge wearers came close and I heard a man's voice exclaim and a woman came running over to see what he had seen. Their voices were muted and mumbled but the woman was clearly arguing that whatever the man was exclaiming was impossible. The woman looked into the tank, we made eye contact for one brief, exposing minute before 'Stasia snapped her eyelids shut. I saw a boot with a sock that pooled around a hairy ankle that terminated before the shin could hit the knee. The boot came forward at my consciousness like a kick in the ass, and there was an impact... and my eyes snapped open once more.

I was back in my bunk bed where I had started, where I had known that my body lay all along. I was moist with a clammy sweat but otherwise nothing was out of the ordinary.

I got up, it was a bit early and everyone else was still sleeping, so I crept out of the room quietly and to the shower with my bar of soap and my towel, my bathrobe wrapped tightly around me as I chilled from my sweat. I washed off and then let the warm water beat down on me. In theory there was unlimited hot water on the space station since everything was reused and energy was plentiful, but it was unusual to get enough time in between training to enjoy it and it was very rare to get time alone in the shower room.

The tiles grew foggy as it misted up. I wondered how far away Anastasia was and how long she had been in that tub of fluid. I wondered how long they planned on keeping her there. I wondered most of all what had been in the center of the blossom that she had wanted to show me but hadn't, what was the secret that she was keeping but knew was important enough that she should have told it to me.

Those uniforms had been strange to me. The symbol on their shoulders was emblazoned on my memory. I thought of it, and kept thinking the word, Duke. Duke project. In the Eye of the Boar. These clues weren't much, but with them it would be possible to find her, perhaps and maybe, if I could figure out where these things were from.

I finished my shower and bundled myself up to go back to my bunk. My roommates were still sound asleep. I fished a notepad out of my tackle trunk and drew the insignia I had seen, tracing out the strange chair-like outline over and over until it looked right. I noted the colors. If I ever came across whatever military or perhaps even private group that wore a uniform like that, I would be able to get some sort of idea of who had my sister and what purpose they might be using her for. My imagination refused to speculate on what those purposes might be and I was grateful to it for being deliberately obtuse on the matter. What I knew of her situation was bad enough without adding wild speculation to it.

I was drying my hair and looking at the drawing I had made when I heard one of my room mates wake up. His name was Azain and he wasn't a bad guy at all.

He had pale blue eyes and dark brown hair and a snubbed up nose that was prone to adenoids and made him sound like he was being a know-it-all even when he wasn't. He was from a neighbourhood only a couple of rungs worse off than my own and he was buying his way into becoming a lieutenant as well. He got pretty rowdy whenever anyone else was around, but when it was quiet like this he let it slip that he was smarter then he acted and a lot nicer too.

"Did I wake you?" I asked, whispering a bit as I did so that I wouldn't wake up everyone else as well before the alarm sounded.

"No. I had a strange dream."

I walked over to his bunk, he was sitting propped up with his head on his hand. I ducked under the bunk and sat beside him, still drying off my hair. It had taken me a little bit to realize that you could act even this comfortable with another human being who wasn't family, but I was coming to enjoy being able to get close to someone else just to talk. I liked how it didn't end up in a goopy clamshell in the morning. That was neat.

"What did you dream about?"

"I dreamt about you."

"You didn't," I laughed, but I felt nervous and a little caught out. Could he be sensitive to Anastasia somehow? Did this increase danger to her or to me?

"I did dream about you. It was weird. I think I watched too much holovision last night."

I calmed down as I realized that he seemed more bemused then concerned by his dream, but I was still cautious. "I hope I wasn't on the evening news!"

I laughed but he barely laughed in return. "It was kind of like that. You were in a field, it was the biggest field I had ever seen, and it was filled with grass that came up to your knee and flowers that were a beautiful blue. You were talking to the wind and the wind was talking to you. You were wearing a dress that billowed in the wind, it was the same blue as the flowers and it reminded me of your eyes and the color of the sky when it's in a movie or another planet."

His statement was oddly intimate and I looked at him closely, realizing that Azain may have a crush on me and I could be encouraging him with my incautious behaviour. Thoughts of the clam shell bed again. I closed my eyes to clear the image from my mind. When I opened them again, his eyes were clear and he looked to me like someone who was still dreaming even though his eyes were open. There was no subtext to his words, he was just telling me his dream as he saw it, nothing more.

"What happened then, Azain?"

He laughed then and the dream fell from him. "Well, then Verily Wrought appeared out of the wind on a pegasus and carried you off into the stars."

He was blushing on his pale skin very badly. The tips of his ears had turned purple red. "Well, I saw Verily Wrought on the news last night, and there was a flying horse for the act at half time during the game."

I felt my own face flame at his observations. I wondered how obvious my crush on Verily Wrought was to my new companions and decided from the sudden light in Azain's eyes that while it hadn't been obvious to him before, it had suddenly become as obvious as the vivid blush across my nose.

As I had feared, Azain was far from discreet about his newly discovered weapon against me. It wasn't that my fellow recruits disliked me, it was just that I had a reputation as being a snob and up until now there hadn't really been anything that they had to pick on me about, at least anything that could get under my skin.

It didn't bother me that they thought I was snobby. I guess I come off that way a lot and even in my own grade and in my own social strata I had been accused of being anywhere from aloof to stuck up. I was also a Field Doctor and had had all sorts of training before we had even met our Sergeant and learned to salute.

I didn't mean to be a snob, but I had several personality traits that counted against me. First of all, I like to read and I love to learn new things. This is a legitimate love of mine, but my peers have always interpreted this as being a brown nose. It was like my work and studies at the infirmary- I was doing it out of interest and a desire to save my life or the life of anyone near me who may become injured. It was a keen interest especially since we were being trained to be sent into very dangerous places and combat zones. This just seems to me to be the sane thing to want to do. If you can learn how to stop bleeding before you're bleeding, well, I think you should really go for it. The other recruits saw this as me getting out of a lot of kitchen duty and many of the repetitive and often physically taxing activities Sarge gave us throughout training.

The second point against me with my new teammates was that I'm also very quiet. I'm not outgoing or bubbly, I don't make a lot of overtures and I would use 'introvert' and 'self-contained' as key descriptors of myself. A lot of people think this is because I'm too busy thinking I'm too good to chat but I'm just not very good at it. I would rather look at people than talk at them. I really like to listen, except when people get loud or rowdy and then I just don't know what to do or how to respond except to make myself quieter.

So the other recruits called me a snob and they said that I was a brown nose and it didn't bother me at all because I understood where they are coming from on those points and honestly, even if I'm not motivated the way they think I am, the end effect is that I do stuff that is both snobby and brown nosing.

Once Azaine found out about my crush... well, after that I never heard the end of it. I mean never, even to this day my crush has become something of a lifestyle for me, and if you read the tabloids you'll know what sort of a joke I'm making about that!

It started off in a kind of radius around Azain. I would walk into a room and the whispering behind hands would begin. Azain would pitch his voice just loud enough for me to hear incidental words like, 'Verily', 'Wrought' and 'Flying Horse'.

We met Sergeant Wommer for the first time the very next day and so we were largely distracted by being told that we were all useless failures and that he couldn't believe he was going to 'be saddled with us group of maggots' for five whole months.

I could not convince people that the story Azain told was his dream. In fact, he told everyone that he had woken me up that morning because I had been talking in my sleep to Verily Wrought and begging him to fly me to his asteroid on his flying horse.

I am not a saint and my embarrassment and anger started to get the better of me. After all, it wasn't fair, it was out and out slander. My only guilt had been the blush across my nose. That was enough and I made it worse by blushing everytime I heard or suspected the story was being repeated by blushing once more, by tightening my shoulders and by turning and leaving the room whenever I could possibly get away with it.

We were all stressed out and I was extremely stressed

out as I was not in very good physical condition and running laps, jumping jack, situps and the dreaded push ups made me the weakest link and I was constantly a target for Wommer's commentary and criticisms. My face was perpetually red from effort and humiliation and my troop took out a lot of their frustration at their own failures with me.

Teasing me encouraged them and it brought their creative cruelty to new heights. It was a game for them to see who could make me blush the most, who could embarrass me the quickest and the hardest. It had been a cruel twist of fate that had made Azain dream a dream that in all honesty I wish I had dreamt myself. It was cruel because I couldn't deny that I wanted Verily Wrought. I had dreamt about him my whole life and in every fantasy, every man who had ever touched me, every kiss I dreamt about, every embrace... yes, it was always Verily's fingers, Verily's lips, Verily's arms around me. It was his voice who whispered, 'Sasha' in the throes of passion and no one but Verily Wrought would ever EVER be good enough for me.

Even Stephen's hypnotic effects on me and the toxic, addictive chemical he excreted was not enough to wipe the yearning I had for the wealthiest man in the galaxy.

And oh, it was so embarrassing. The sheer prideful arrogance that Sasha Wheaton could be destined to become Sasha Wrought. I didn't even know him, it was all an unhealthy, sick and fantastic delusion that I could not and would not shake. Somehow Azain had broken me wide open and now I was fodder for them all.

The funny thing is that after the cruel mocking and teasing started, I actually started to make friends.

Before the whole 'Wrought and the Flying Horse' debacle I had been somewhat untouchable from the rest of the cadets. Suddenly I had been brought down to their level and now I had friends despite the common knowledge that I had had an affair with the station's alien doctor and had a medical degree of my own as a result. Suddenly, I was relateable and slowly I noticed the small courtesies that they paid me for my humiliation. They would try to help out so I wouldn't be the last one to finish my laps every time. Their laughter was underscored with tips and even, sometimes, encouragement.

A'donna was my first real friend. She was older than most of the recruits but even so, she was not going to be an officer. She was an enlisted soldier and she wasn't very strong but she was kind, even if she wasn't too bright. She had run away from her husband who hit her and made her have children even though the children kept dying. She had lost five babies within the first six months of birth and she had terrible nightmares about four of them who had been dreadfully mutated. I had several free hours one afternoon and had gone to have a nap. I woke up abruptly to see Adonna sitting at the foot of my bunk bed. She was sitting cross legged, her fist under her jaw, her eyes bright with interest.

When she saw I was awake she whispered to me. "Were you dreaming of the little red-head? Were you dreaming of the Verily boy?"

I covered my face with my pillow and moaned in mortification but Adonna didn't understand the meaning of shame and she bounced at the foot of my bed happily.

"I knew it! You were dreaming of him! I could tell, you were smiling so sweetly in your sleep!"

Then she tried to take my pillow from me and for the first time in my life I wrestled with a light spirit with someone who wasn't my sister.

After that my person seemed less sacrosanct to the other recruits. Of course, basic training and Sarge's animosity towards me continued to help with that as well.

We were awoken early and had to memorize what the meals for the day were after having a quick shower and usual while cleaning up our rooms so that it would be up to specification.

There was quite a bit of nakedness in front of each other. Men or women, it didn't matter. We were in rooms together and it was expected that everyone would behave themselves. The actual reason we were given for the mixed quarters however was simply that we all needed to get used to it, that GAF didn't have time or capacity to provide separate facilities for everyone on every mission. If we got used to it now it was less likely to bother us later. It also saved discrimination problems with genderless aliens or anyone else who might be offended. It was good business to make sure that we all just tried to act like adults.

It was a good tactic because I had always been painfully shy. Being naked in the locker room for gym class had been more exhausting than gym class as I rushed to put on my clothes in a corner where none of the other girls could see what I was up to. Strutting around naked wasn't really done by any of the exhibitionists because there wasn't enough time for it. We had to shower and get dressed while focussing on what we were memorizing and get it all done in twenty minutes.

Before I knew it I was too busy to be self conscious and I was running across the room with my top off to put the sock away that was hanging off the top shelf and would get us all in trouble during inspection. Then I realized that nobody else was giving me a second glance about it, not even Adain. He was staring at the menu card and muttering under his breath. He noticed my look and smiled distractedly and returned to buttoning up his shirt.

When it was time to return to the shower at the end of the day, I was too stiff and sore and dirty to care about who looked at me in the shower either. I had lost all sense of humiliation at my naked body and it was no different now to me than my clothed body, except often colder.

Our first day we were told what was to be expected of us

and how to salute properly. Then we learned how to do pushups properly. By the end of that I was ready to die. After that they made us run around the oval in the gymnasium again and again. I lost track of how many times it was. It seemed to go on forever.

The next day our rooms were inspected after we dressed and showered and had had breakfast. Then we were told everything wrong we had done and made to fix it. Sarge then messed it up again... and told us to fix it again. Then they repeated this for awhile more. After that we did more pushups and then were herded thought the station's hallways like a troop of baboons and told to run around the oval some more while our C.O's all had lunch on the side lines and goaded us to go faster.

Lunch was pretty late and we were told tomorrow we would have to recite information about the meals of the day before we would be allowed to sit down to eat.

After lunch we were issued our basic equipment and taken on a tour of the different holorooms where much of the training would take place.

The space station around Dalton that was utilized by the Galactic Armed Forces was pretty advanced, it was set up with detailed training facilities including rock walls to climb, a small lake for water maneuvers, about an acre of simulated 'desert' and sand dunes (with the heat cranked up in there and machinery to generate sandstorms we figured it would be our least favourite training room!) and a swampy area for training in

114

adverse conditions.

By our second week we were pretty innured to the endless loops around the oval, push ups, jumping jacks, repeating endless regulations and rules at the drop of a hat. Memorization was a major part of those first week. Finally the regs started to stick as any mistakes resulted in doing pushups over an index card with the correct recitation on it. Each push up would give enough of a glimpse to read it out and then we would have to repeat it until the C.O thought we had it down enough. Jumping to my feet I would gasp out the correct regulation and be permitted to return to my previous activity.

Learning how to clean and assemble various guns and other GAF issue weaponry while trying not to watch Sergeant Wommer prowling around and pouncing on the other recruits was enough to make me sweat buckets. The apprehension of it was enough to make you forget every regulation and any other fragment of learning in your mind. I was no longer the one he picked on for everything and I couldn't help but think everytime, 'better them than me.'

The nervousness that crippled me was enough to make me tremble when my C.O. Came near me. He seemed to feed off my nervousness and preyed on me more than the others, or so it seemed to me. Later on many of the others told me that they felt targeted by him especially as well.

It was a strange thing, because between him yelling at me, the exercise, the punishments that resulted in less and less sleep and food, a cloudy fugue descended over my mind. I became too tired to jump at the sound of his voice anymore. Suddenly barking out the answer became a very effecient method of dealing with this omnipresent threat in my life. My fear responses were being proven to me, even on a cellular level to be a misguided and wrong. Suddenly, I found myself dealing with threats head on.

Chapter 5: I Get Guns

"I love firing guns. It's an amazing feeling – so sexy and powerful."
-Hayley Atwell

     I had never seen a gun up close, not any closer than in a holster on Sargeant any rate. Before that I had seen them in the holos and on the news, holstered by a cop or a security guard across the street, but I had certainly never held one before.

     The GAF had a wide range in weaponry but most of the weapons available to raw recruits were from the Wrought Munitions Econo-Safe line. They weren't like a lot of the ones that I had seen on movies, but they were similar to most of the ones on the news. Big, bulky and with a lot of things that moved on them. Each gun, laser or other device had a manual that came with it and a large section on trouble shooting.

This was the first time that the complaints about the legendary GAF cheapness became evident to me. Equipment was not a top priority for the GAF. They had standard issue and then anything that you wanted above that would cost you. I wondered if I should have saved my commission for weapons upgrades instead but it was too late to wonder about 'what ifs'. The GAF had my money and that was final.

The lightest of the smaller Econo-Safe guns weighed fifteen pounds. The first time I tried to fire the TrailBLazer 5000 it lit up and I felt a powerful thrum go through the machine and then it went prrrrffffm and a little tiny cloud of smoke came up from it. Sarge said that this was likely to happen in the field as well and that was why it was important to memorize the entire trouble shooting section. I dejectedly took my misfiring weapon over to the table where Reid and Tapping were working on the same thing at a metal table. I moved a bit further away when I noticed the trickle of smoke still coming out of the barrel of Reid's gun.

Tapping was reading the words with her finger and mouthing them, her progress was slow. I opened it up to the Trouble Shooting section and understood quickly why. The Trouble Shooting section was highly technical and assumed that you had a thorough understanding not only of the names and locations of each part and moveable piece on the gun, but also that you understood their function and relation to the rest of the gun, to yourself and to your target. It used words like 'haffle' and 'scusluslinger' in a casual way that was alarming to me.

118

This was only one weapon. I hoped that they had some parts in common because if we had to memorize different parts on each weapon before being able to access the trouble shooting guide I was pretty sure that we were going to have an extremely high mortality rate.

By the end of the first day, I hadn't managed to get a single shot fired.

It was not only extremely depressing, it was also worrying for the future. I started to scan any possible way that I could earn a bit of extra money for some improved weapons for myself. Nothing reputeable was coming to mind. None of us talked that night, I think that we were all having the same thoughts about our own mortality.

We all left our bunk lights on and I could hear everyone else flipping through the books, whispered pronunciations punctuated the flippings from the front couplee of pages where the parts were diagramed and to the back third of the book that was all the trouble shooting pages. There were a lot of reasons that a gun could misfire and not all of them could be fixed on the spot. At the end of a long list of possible tweaks, alterations and other equipment suggestions, nearly every last suggestion was, 'call customer support'.

The lack of decent equipment in the GAF appeared to be a problem that everyone accepted, sympathized with and told you to deal with. The only answer in the end was to have cold, hard credits on hand to purchase upgraded models, or just ones that worked. I decided that I was probably better off using the TrailBLazer 5000 as a club and that was when my trouble shooting paid off.

The bolt of energy that came out was brilliant cherry red and smelled hot and jagged in my nose. I fired it at the targets a few more times and the smell of burning faded some. I grinned at Sarge who grinned back and gave me a big two thumbs up. I took another shot at the target and seared the shoulder of it off. This was fun.

Pfffffffmpshhmm

And my gun was out of comission again. Sarge shrugged at me and pointed to the metal table. That's where everyone else was sitting already. It was getting crowded.

Sarge was like a different man while all this was going on. He didn't yell at any of his, he would scan through on the trouble shooting guide with one large finger and flip back to the front when we had been stuck on one problem for too long. Our guns weren't all the same and the parts weren't all named the same way. This was going to be a big problem.

After a week of hit or miss shooting, mostly miss, we came to one conclusion, we all needed better guns. Nothing was going to fix these ones.

120

The little weasly guy that we all called, 'Scrawny', finally came up with an idea for better guns.

"Wet t-shirt contest."

"That's not fair. Only us girls can earn money doing wet t-shirts," Tapping was indignant.

Scrawny shook his head. "Yes, I mean, no, you don't know that. People would pay money to dump cold water on my head. I'd just have to keep talking to them and they'd be grateful for the chance to shut me up."

Rich nodded. "Some days I'd be happy to trade in a better gun for myself if I could dump some water on his head."

Tapping leaned into the conversation excitedly. "I bet I could do the same thing. I could be really annoying."

"You're all really annoying," Rumbled Feldmore. We all ignored him.

"How would we earn money with wet t-shirts?" I asked quietly.

Niblet answered earnestly, "Oh, it's really easy,

121

everyone who wants in has to pay a fee for each bucket. They rate us and judge us and the water keeps coming while we all make a big deal about how cold the water is and then afterwards we split the money between us no matter who wins... although, sometimes it's also for charity."

Rich grinned. "You sure know a lot about this, Niblet."

She blushed and grabbed a couple of chips out of a bowl and started munching on them while glaring at Rich, but she didn't really look that mad. It occurred to me that she was actually flirting a bit with Rich and he certainly was looking at her awfully close.

Scrawny interjected again. "She's got the right idea, we can ask if we can charge a cover fee too. If they will give us a cut of the cover charge we might only have to do this once."

"We might have to do it more than once?" I asked. This whole idea sounded awfully public.

"Well, we'll have to snoop around and do some market testing."

I nodded in Sarge's direction, he was looking through his french fries as though they could be harbouring snipers.

"Someone is going to have to ask Sarge for permission to do this. I think it could take us a couple of days to get everything set up and we aren't supposed to be able to leave until we have a leave day.

Silent eyes looked over at me. I narrowed my own eyes back and put a carrot stick down in disgust. "Fine. I'll go talk to him."

I walked over to Sarge and saluted. Nobody ever sought Sarge out and I was a little shaky on the proper etiquette in how to talk to him under these new terms where he didn't yell an insult at me first.

"At ease, cadet. What's on your mind?"

"We've been talking, Sir... and I, we that is came up with an idea to earn some money for new weapons." I felt really lame talking to him about this. I felt like I was some sort of grifter angling for a desperate need.

"Oh, you did, did you? What did you guys come up with?"

He didn't seem surprised but rather blandly curious about what our plan was.

"Well, up, Scrawny had the idea... that is, he suggested um, a wet t-shirt contest."

He set down his fork. He looked up at me, his eyebrows lifted. "Well, that's not a half bad idea."

He looked me up and down appraisingly and I blushed. He looked moderately impressed. "Yeah, that should be alright. Last guys through just had a bake sale, but I think this is a much better idea."

"A bake sale?"

"Yes, it was quite the ordeal though, I wouldn't suggest it and the upgrades they were able to afford were only barely worth the investment and time."

"Does everyone wind up buying new guns?"

"Everyone but the stupidest ones."

"Maybe a bake sale wouldn't be a bad-"

"I like your idea better. Go with that one."

"Yeah?"

He nodded and started putting apple crumble into his mouth. He looked up at me standing and staring at him still. He shooed me away with his hands and glowered and then returned to his pie.

"He didn't yell," Reid was excited

"What did he say?"

"He said 'yes'... and it sounds like everyone does this... or, not something exactly like this, but something to raise money for upgrades. Nobody uses our training weapons for anything unless they are idiots."

Scrawny grinned knowingly. "Wrought Munitions know how to get more money, that's for sure. They sell guns that nobody in their right mind would ever use in combat but GAF pays for them, saves themselves a bunch of money and anyone who isn't happy with it can upgrade."

Tapping kicked him. "Don't encourage Wrought, they're trying to get us all killed."

Feldmore scowled. "Wrought isn't here. Who cares."

125

Felger raised a hand as though asking permission to speak. "Actually, my father was involved in the advertising department on Dalton, and all the intercom speakers in any public area and most private ones are wired to activate when key words, like 'Wrought' or other brands are used. All the surrounding information is fed into Central Data and registered into general feedback..."

Rich grinned. "Wrought sucks your mother's balls, Felger."

Felger folded his arms. "Very funny, Rich."

"Could we just talk about the wet t-shirt contest. I don't care who hears that these guns are crap. I don't want to die reading the trouble shooting section of my operating manual. I want a weapon that works."

"They should ship these things off to our enemies. Rebels or something as a charity donation. They'd all be dead before dinner," Feldmore's voice was a rumble in his chest.

"How do you know they don't do that, too?" Scrawny asked.

Getting ready for a wet t-shirt contest was easier than I thought it would be. Sarge opened a locker that had been locked up until now and removed large, stiff sheets of paper and markers. It really did seem that this was part of weapons training: Fundraising 101.

I had never been exposed to a wet t-shirt contest but Scrawny and Tapping both seemed to have a fair idea of how it should go. Scrawny talked to the owner of the bar on Martial 43 and we gave up training on the TrailBLazer 5000s all together. They were just a message from Wrought Industries that you needed to learn how to fundraise.

Our first job, after Scrawny got the enthusiastic go ahead from the owner of the bar, was to make posters. There was going to be a cover charge and even though there was some protesting from myself and Reid, Scrawny had scheduled two nights in a row for our t-shirt spectacular. The boys were going to participate as well. Feldmore was really built, Scrawny thought that he might legitimately attract some women who might want to dump some cold water on him. Azain and Felger were a little less... intriguing, but Scrawny had that mouth on him and he was pretty sure he could heckle people into buying a lot of buckets of water to dump over his head.

Felger offered to be the Master of Ceremonies and Rich would take the money. Of course, Nibleworth, Reid, Tapping and myself were the main attractions. As it came up to time to go we all felt a little nervous, even Tapping. I think we were all mainly worried that no one would show up. We really needed our guns.

We went through a back set of tunnels that Scrawny had discovered with the help of the bar owner so that we wouldn't have to go through the main corridors of the space station. Our posters had attracted a fair number of people into the bar, we knew that they were there for us by the cheers that went up when we showed up on the stage at the front of the bar.

Scrawny went to the front with us and so did Feldmore and they were hooted at by a crowd of women who seemed to have all come in together. They waved some credits in the air at Scrawny and Feldmore. Feldmore was blushing down to the neck of his white t-shirt but Scrawny was bowing and strutting around the stage like a wrestler or a rockstar. I blushed on his behalf. My hands were balled up into nervous fists.

Rich had a bucket of credits by the front door and he was standing by the two burly bouncers who were also collecting the cover charge he grinned at us standing on the stage and gave us a thumbs up. I could see the blue credits cresting the top of the bucket even at that distance. We were going to get some awesome weapons.

The wet t-shirt contest wasn't too bad after all. I was really nervous when the first guy picked me out to soak with the big red bucket of water. He was a large, ruddy faced, dark haired young man who was clearly already somewhat drunk. He put a blue twenty-five credit into the bucket at Felger's feet and with a huge grin threw it in my face. I shrieked and turned away a bit and the audience laughed and gave a few token 'boos'.

I got the message, they wanted to hit me full frontal. The next guy picked me as well and waggled his forefinger at me warningly. I nodded and squeezed my eyes shut. He hit me full in the face and the crowd cheered.

I don't think I was the only one who was surprised to see how true to his word Scrawny had been about being selected based off of his loud mouth and skinny frame. It wasn't just the men either, the women picked on him too. At the end of the night he was declared the winner based off of him having the most buckets chosen to have dumped on him. I was in awe. Nibles was second and I was third. Feldmore placed last and that seemed to irritate him beyond all reason. It wasn't like it was fun having water dumped in your face repeatedly, although, it hadn't actually *not* been fun...

We went back to our rooms late that night and sat together in the central atrium with our buckets of credits. We counted it out and discovered that we had enough for our target guns: the Sniper Blaster Six. It had a wide range of sniper capacity as well as a machine gun setting and worked off of three types of ammo and three types of lasers. It was reviewed very well according to 'Sniper Review' and it was the most affordable weapon in its class. In addition, we also had enough for one extra smaller auxillary weapon for half of us. We decided to put on the show for the second night was we had agreed on with the bar owner.

The second night was even more crowded and we stood on the stage until we were all shivering and had to stop.

We didn't have to wake up early either morning, Sarge told us to do what we had to do and then we would go back to weapons training once we went down to the store and picked up our new weaponry. We all agreed that we would trust the money to my locker over night and count it in the morning.

In the morning we spread the credits out on the floor. We had collected a lot of blue credits, but there were wads of yellow credits and the occasional red or even purple credits mixed in. I had been more confident and placed second that night, Scrawny still beat me out of first place. Nibleworth and Reid had tied. Tapping had placed last this time and Feldmore was both smug that he wasn't last and grouchy that he had to work so hard for second to last place.

We had definitely done better last night than the night before. We had enough money now for our sidearms, knives, and most amazingly of all, light weight flack vests for us all. We couldn't afford the ones that could hold out laser fire, but keeping shrapnel out was a good deal considering our other option weighed sixty pounds and wasn't guaranteed against anything over small ballistic fire. We were all very happy.

We were a lot happier when we came back to Sarge and showed off our new weaponry. He said that it was much better than the last group had done with their bake sale. He was chuckling a lot and Nibleworth and I both blushed. He had made a trip to the bar himself and paid out some credits into our fund. Nibleworth and I had both gotten nailed by him.

Sarge showed us how to use our new guns. We went through the owners manual but the trouble shooting sections were a lot shorter and so then it was down to actually learning how to get some accuracy with the things and switch between single shot function to machine gun spray and also into sniper mode. I was surprised that I was a good shot and sometimes I'd jump up and grin when I hit the target dead center. Sarge had stopped being quite so lenient with us after we had gained our new weaponry but he grinned back at me anyhow and gave me the thumbs up again. That small sign of approval from Sarge was worth gold.

We started drilling with the Sniper Blasters and learning how to use our handguns. We weren't a wealthy group of cadets but nobody could say we weren't resourceful.

We were all becoming soldiers, and no one was more surprised than me. When we were introduced to the Swamp Room I didn't feel anything more than trepidation and caution. I stood unflinching as the Sarge barked out our orders to us and gave us a quick overview of our new challenge.

Chapter 6: The Swamp

"My coming of faith did not start with a leap but rather a series of staggers from what seemed like one safe place to another. Like lily pads, round and green, these places summoned and held me while I grew. Each prepared me or the next leaf on which I would land, and in this way I moved across the swamp of doubt and fear."
-Anne Lamott

The Swamp Room could be set to blistering muggy heat or to freezing so that you were constantly falling through the thin ice on it and left with blue freezing lips. It was our Sarge's idea of training to put us at one end of The Swamp, set it to smoldering, and tell us to get to the other end while he went off for a cold drink.

Our first time through the swamp was difficult for us. We were all loaded down with heavy packs and equipment. I had two pots that had been attached to my designated pack and they clanged together loudly and were constantly startling me. Hummocks drifted through the swamp and the water varied in depth if you weren't able to find a handy tussock anywhere from ankle deep to past my eyes and suddenly I was trying to swim with ninety pounds of gear on my back. We were all grateful for the lighter weaponry and armour. I don't think I could have moved loaded down the way we had been outfitted.

Up until now, except for our fundraising sidebar, we hadn't been asked to do anything that involved trying to think, it had kind of seemed to me as though they were actually trying to train us out of the habit of thinking. Now we had to do something other than pushups or wet t-shirt contests. Getting across this swamp was going to require a bit of brain.

There was the heat, the humidity and the flights of gnats that were locked into the simulator to seek out humans relentlessly. Felger's glasses fogged up repeatedly. He wiped them off and cursed them. I felt bad for him about that, eye surgery would be an important expense for him so that he didn't need glasses. It was our first time with the fully loaded packs as well as being in a strange terrain and that was only a part of our problems.

There was also the gumbo. It was black and thick and sucked off one of my boots before I was able to extricate myself. We were a sorry group when we reached to exit that first day. I was covered in mud and soaking wet. I lost points for losing my boot and it took us over five hours to get most of us across the room and then we realized that we had forgot Midge somewhere in the swamp and Sergeant Wommer sent us back in with a tongue lashing. We found her sunk in the mud up to her nose and had to form a human chain in order to yank

133

her out of the mud. She was so covered in gumbo that even after she was out of the mud she could barely move and we had to drag her to the finish and then into the shower where we turned the water on to warm and let it hose her down in all her gear and clothes until she could move enough to start getting out of it on her own.

I think that I can speak for my entire troop when I say we were each and everyone of us glad to not have had it be me who had to be dragged out of the swamp so ignominiously.

The next day we went back to the swamp room and where last time we had all started across the acre size space very independently of each other, this time we hesitated before starting out. There was more then one person who glanced at Midge, myself included. A lot of people glanced at her to see if she was going to fail again, to try to judge if she was the weak link of the group, but I looked at her because I was worried that this time tomorrow, I was going to *be* her.

I have never been very strong or athletic and when I had found the deep water the day before I had come perilously close myself to getting stuck. Now I was wondering if this time I would be the one to be left behind and force everyone to come back and haul my ass out of the muck. I was understandably worried. All the pushups in the world were never going to make me confident in facing physical challenges. I knew I needed other people to help me.

The part of my mind that had once been obsessed with

134

fear was now obsessed with survival. It had become much more detached and cynical from the jibbering wreckage that it had once been. It was that part of my brain that showed me that I needed other people, that I had to learn to be a team player... and it was that part of me that showed me that currently, I had no one but myself.

Our Unit was not a unit. We were not anywhere near a team. A few of us had become friends but at that point we hadn't even really had long enough to form a decent clique or two. In fact, I think it was safe to say that there were only one or two of us who even remembered any names unless we were being yelled at by Sarge, then we could remember anything. Our time at the wet t-shirt contest had been a sudden sprint of group brilliance and it gave me hope and I think it made me just a little brave.

I wasn't meaning to be brave and step forward at that point, in fact, in my mind I was being cowardly. After all, I only said something because I didn't want to be the one in Midge's place tomorrow. The only camraderie we shared was in our group feeling of being hard done by and unique from our Sergeant in that he was the oppressor and we were his victims... But our weapons and our armour showed something else, something better in us all.

I didn't really know them and I wouldn't have chosen them, but I had a need to survive.

"I think we should stay together." I ventured. My voice sounded thin to my ears and seven sets of eyes turned to look at me.

I tried again. "I think we should stay together. No one is allowed to leave until we all get to the exit anyway, it isn't a race. If we all help out we can go for lunch sooner."

I looked at the other faces. They had formed a rough circle while I spoke.

Midge was the first to speak, her brown hair was already plastered against her head from the swamp's humidity.

"I'll second that," she said. "I think this room is monitored so that someone would have stepped in if the mud had gone any higher but... I was pretty freaked out. I wouldn't want anyone else to go through that... or for me to have to go through that again."

Azain nodded his agreement. I was relieved because the others seemed to look to Azain somewhat for leadership. Adonna, who previously had just been 'Reid', Ron Felger, again, previously 'Felger', Guido Scrazzonatti, Sarge called him 'Scrawny', and Stan 'Rich' Richardson nodded as well. Feldmore folded his arms skeptically however. Midge Nibleworth, who we had always called, 'Niblet' previously was visibly agitated.

"Feldmore, if you don't want to stay with the group, you can go on your own, but I'm not sure why it would matter to you."

Feldmore was the biggest in our Unit. He folded his arms and took a step towards me. I looked up at him but didn't step back.

"I don't like to get slowed down."

Guido took a step forward. "Well, if we're slowing you down, get chopping."

Feldmore looked at the group of people who had spontaneously decided to actually become a group and then turned with a snort and headed out across the swamp. We watched him leave for a minute. I wasn't the only one shaking my head. It really wasn't a race.

That was when we all introduced ourselves on our own terms. Previously, we were always either exhausted or had Sarge breathing down our necks. There were also a lot of differences in social strata between all of us. These differences were part of survival on Dalton and they were insidiously inlaid in our collective subconscious. They had also kept us from gelling as a group.

Everyone was from Dalton, of course, but it turned out that Guido, the two time winner of the wet t-shirt contest, had come to Dalton with his family when he was fourteen and he was originally from Old Earth. He suddenly rose in my esteem. I knew it was irrelevant but it was thrilling to think he had walked on the soil of the same planet as many of the historical people I had read about. Dalton had very little human history and even less of a human future in store for it. Where Dalton was bleak, Old Earth was rich, she was layered and fragrant.

I learned everyone's first name then except for Feldmore. For all of basic training he would always be Feldmore to us all and I still can't remember his first name.

"So, what's our plan?" Adonna Reid asked.

"I think just go tussock to tusscok as much as we can, if anyone gets stuck in the muck we help them out," Azaine said, surveying the distance to the exit as he did.

It was really not very far at all. It should have been so easy, but progress yesterday had taken us forever and every boot sucking footstep was an exercise in slow motion. The tussocks were too small generally for more than one person to step on so we had to go in a line.

We learned quickly that Guido was the best at spotting what ground could hold the weight of a person and what couldn't. He was from small and wiry Italian stock and he was

138

quicker than the eye when it came to pulling away from danger. If ground turned out to be unstable he would dart back before we could blink and off to try another course.Going as a group was at first a bit slower because we all had to wait while Guido spelunked ahead and found the most stable ground for us to cross.

Feldmore had taken a direct route across the room and he was splashing across the water without looking for ground to stand on. He was well over six feet and built like a bull. He also didn't seem to mind the filthy water and seemed to be relying on sheer momentum to get him through the gumbo.

Watching him, I could see why he was worried about being slowed down. He weighed more than any of us and getting bogged down could become a big problem for him if he did anything rather than charge ahead. It was possible or even likely that Guido's path wouldn't have worked for Feldmore's larger mass either.

I was taking up the rear and so I had a fair bit of time to watch Feldmore make his way across the swamp, I also saw when he got into trouble and his momentum failed him. I tapped Azain on the shoulder, he was ahead of me. He saw Feldmore as well and shook his head.

"What should we do?"

"I don't know. Let's try to get us all across, we're too far away to help him and there aren't any easy paths out to him, we'd pretty much have to swim and muck hop our way over there."

"I hope he gets himself free. He's such a big guy, I don't know how any of us'd even help him get unstuck."

I nodded in agreement. It was tempting to wish that he wouldn't get free just to teach him a lesson, but more than anything else, I really wanted to get out of the swamp and to an early lunch. I was supposed to spend the afternoon in the infirmary and I had had a bit of a yearning to see Stephen again. I wondered a little if it was because I had run out of syrup, but I think I was just lonely and tired. My need to see him and be held was powerful and I didn't want to end up spending most of the day on this acre of muck.

We continued across from hummock to hummock. The process was far from perfect and none of us were dry by the time we made it to the little grassy rise that terminated into a cement wall with a red 'exit' sign over top of the crash bar. I had fallen in to my waist, but I had both boots this time and my pack was mostly dry which made a big difference in weight and comfort. Even Guido had fallen in and his left leg was wet to his crotch and both of his boots sloshed with swamp water.

Then there was Feldmore. He had only made it a couple of feet past where Azain and I had first spotted him struggling and he was up to his chin in mud and water now. Guido was emptying his boots and sitting on the grass watching him and our elation was mitigated as we all watched him sinking slowly deeper in the muck.

Midge's eyes were large with empathy. "We can't leave him out there."

"I wouldn't want to slow him down." Adonna's lips were held in a bitter sneer. I didn't like the way it made her normally attractive face look and I frowned.

Guido snorted. "Of course we can't leave him out there, if we do, we'll never get lunch."

At the base of it, that was just the truth. The exit looked like it was only a few feet away, but it was as far away as the distance to Feldmore and back. Guido finished lacing up his sodden boots once more.

"I'll go see if I can find a path to get him out. It'll be easier if I scout it out first to see what, if anything we can do next."

"What do you mean, 'if anything'?" Midge asked, her voice high and nervous, I was still trying to decide if Nibles fit her better than her birth name, Midge. It was a close call.

None of us bothered to answer her, even though she was just afraid and identifying with her scare from the day

141

before. We didn't bother to answer her because she was panicking and had forgotten that this was, after all, just a training exercise. Our C.O. Wasn't going to leave Feldmore to die in a fake swamp just to prove to us that we ought to be more of team. We weren't trained properly yet and even if a real life situation, with training and only the resources on hand, it was highly likely that we wouldn't be able to get a big guy like that out of the jam he'd gotten himself into. He hadn't acted like it was a real situation with real dangers and that was the whole point of the training rooms. If he couldn't keep cool without any actual pressure on him, how would he do when he was out in the real world, in real combat?

Guido ran with all considerable lithenes at his disposal across the swamp. It wasn't an easy track to Feldmore and he was covered in mud and muck himself by the time he was close. He knelt down on a tussock about eight feet away from Feldmore. He was talking to him but we couldn't hear what he said. Feldmore had sunk down past his mouth now and was responding with muffled hums and eye motions from what we could see. Guido shook his head and held out his hands, shrugging his shoulders. On our safe hill we all glanced at each other. It didn't look good.

Guido came back quicker then he had gone out. "Unless someone has a brilliant idea, I think we should knock on the door and ask for help. I think he's only got five, maybe ten minutes before the mud covers his nose."

There was no solid ground, no coveniently placed anything to place a rope. It was way to far to use the little hill as solid ground to operate from.

"I think we should knock."

I was the one who had spoken and I was the one who knocked. I had barely rapped on the door when our C.O. And eight others came pouring into the Swamp. They were equipped with a small boat and a harness. I saw that one of them carried a little oxygen tank. They put the oxygen tank on Feldmore as soon as they reached him. It was fortunate they had come in when they did since he sunk below his nose shortly after the mask was put on him. I couldn't imagine how it must feel, like being buried alive. His eyes peered out at us. Soon they would be under that mucky quicksand too.

It took them twenty minutes to extricate Feldmore.

After they had rescued Feldmore, they had let him have enough time with an oxygen tank and a thermal equalization blanket to make sure that he was alright. I watched Stephen monitoring the vital signs while we all stood at attention, facing the swamp and covered in mud, waiting.

Finally Stephen nodded at Sarge and the other officers who had come in as well, many of whom I had never seen before. I realized with regret that this was probably all I was going to see of Dr. Johnson today. He hadn't even made eye contact with me or nodded to let me know he noticed me.

"On your feet, Soldier!" Sarge barked at Feldmore. I felt a surge of empathy for him as he staggered a bit, still completely caked with mud, his eyes looked foggy and indistinct.

It had just gone downhill from there.

Feldmore collapsed in a muddly pile. The strapped him to a stretcher and then he was taken to be hosed off. I found out later that afternoon when I was doing my shift in the medical wing that he had had to be sedated when he woke up screaming and thrashing.

Meanwhile, all of us except Feldmore were made to run around the halls in our mud covered boots. Sargeant Wommer was left with Feldmore in the swamp room while Captain Wood monitored our run in our heavy boots. We left mud splatters everywhere, even on the ceiling. After we had run to exhaustion we were made to clean the mess we had made, but we weren't permitted to change or get clean so it was nearly impossible to mop up the muck without making more of a mess.

Niblet started to cry in fatigue and frustration and Wood sent her to do pushups on the part of the floor she had managed to clean. I'm still not sure what lesson we were supposed to learn from this except that letting a fellow soldier die left a big, hard to clean mess and you were stuck with dirty hands.

Hmmm, I think maybe I did learn what they were trying to teach us after all.

I didn't know how to feel about what had happened with Feldmore. I wondered if it was my fault, or if it was all our faults for not insisting he come with the group. Of course, it's impossible to make someone play on a team if they don't want to play on a team. That's what they try to teach you in training,but some people will never learn it.

Feldmore was one of these people.
He wasn't injured physically from his foray into the swamp and the next day we were put into the same environment all over again. Anyone with half a brain and a spot of humility in them would have learned the lesson and put their 'independence' away.

That's the thing about arrogance, it doesn't matter how humiliating the failure, how low someone sinks in the mud... in this case very literally, they refuse to learn from their mistakes. Learning would mean that at one point, they had been wrong, and that would just be too much for a delicate ego to handle.

Feldmore certainly didn't look like he had a delicate ego, but he hid behind his hulking facade and his handsome yet too thick features. He was still a little boy and he had to have things his own way. After seeing Feldmore rescued, none of the rest of us wanted to risk being a maverick and the very first thing we all did was to group up after we entered the training arena.

145

Feldmore sulked to one side, pretending to be checking his straps... but looking over at us furtively. It was frustrating because he was even more aloof from the group than he had been the day before. Midge hated conflict and she kept looking over at Feldmore and fiddling with her own straps on her bag in some sort of sympathetic reaction. Feldmore saw her looks and deliberately turned more of his back to us.

"They won't let us leave if he doesn't finish," Guido pitched his voice quietly but I sensed Feldmore tense. He was way too nervous, way too... touchy. The situation with Feldmore had gone from irritating to volatile for us witnessing his humilation.

We were all smarting from Sarge's dressing down of us as a group collectively and of Feldmore was smarting specifically. Come to think of it, after the way Sarge screamed at Feldmore it wasn't really surprising he was touchy. None of us had come off squeaky clean in the training thus far. It was clear from how much angry spittle had coated all of us that we were not impressing our local GAF representative, i.e. Sarge. He was not at all happy with how we were gelling as a group.

None of us disliked Feldmore, I had never seen anyone teasing him or anything, the guy just wasn't very friendly and none of us were secure enough to make him feel secure enough t to join in with us.

I've really come to believe that most people, with the exception of some real psychos, would prefer to be accepted

146

into any group dynamic they come across. It's a very basic need humans all have for survival and we all intuit that if a group accepts us, it's good, and if they don't, it could be very very bad. Let me put it this way, unless people have your back, they're likely to knife you in it.

It's not always a cruel thing either, or a vicious one. It's just expedient. For example, if Guido were in trouble and Feldmore was in trouble as well, I would help Guido first. There are several reasons for this: the first one is that he would probably physically be closer to me to rescue because he wasn't being a douche like Feldmore and deliberately keeping his distance from me and the rest of the group. Let's say that he was close to me physically, even closer to me than Guido, well, I'd still rescue Guido. I'd do it for a lot of reasons, but one of the biggest reasons is that I *know* that he'd rescue me in the situation, but who knows about Feldmore. He's an unknown quantity and could do pretty much anything.

Of course, if I rescued Guido and Feldmore was still sitting there, needing rescue, I'd run right over and help him anyway he'd let me, but at that point... it could be too late for our non-group member.

This brings it back to Feldmore, deliberately turning his back on us, acting like a pathetic Maverick wannabe, too proud to come over and say, 'what's up, guys?'. Why would he act that way when his life could quite conceivably depend on us one day?

Well, it's because he's scared of being rejected. I got to know him a bit better over the next few months, and I learned that this is a pattern of almost all rejects. They are rejects because they are afraid of being rejected and this way, the Feldmores of the world retain a degree of power over the rejection process.

None of us were privy to these deep truths of group dynamics and so at that point all of us were nursing hurt feelings of rejection ourselves. He had successfully taken 'the power' for himself and it had left us feeling like he was a big jerk. Meanwhile, Feldmore's situation wasn't improved from the previous day and the dressing down he got from Sarge at all.

Feldmore was a bit more circumspect this time. He didn't charge right through the swamp but he refused to have anything to do with the rest of us, either. Since we had Guido with us we had an immediate advantage in the room because even though everything was different in the swamp room, he could see a path through it as clearly laid out as a walking trail in a park for you and me.

Feldmore stubbornly refused to use anything even obliquely connected to our path, he was rather effectively shunning us and it was absolutely to his own detriment and not at all a detriment to us, except for giving Midge and then by infection, me, a case of the nervous giggles. He looked really funny, wrapping his way around the room, up to his armpits in the muck rather than use a tussock Guido selected. He looked like a jerk.

148

We got to the far side of the room and the promise of hot showers and Sarge walked through the door.

"Attention!"

We were all pretty tired but we snapped to, all except for Feldmore who was still struggling along behind. He did a lot better this time, I mean, compared to last time which was absolutely horrible. He wasn't too far behind, but we all stood at attention while Sarge smirked at us all and most especially smirked at Feldmore. We all stood there, at attention until Feldmore struggled out of the swamp and stood at the end of our ever so slightly ragged line and snapped to attention.

"Dismissed."

We all turned, I could barely escape the room in time, neither could the others who practically tripped on my heels. We weren't even tired anymore, just grateful that we weren't going to get yelled at today and rushing to make sure that we escaped any possible ambush from Captain Wood and more hellish tasks.

Sarge grabbed Feldmore by the shoulder. "Not you, son."

The door closed on its pneumatic slide behind us without a chance for us to hear anything that Sarge said to Feldmore. Whatever he said, and whatever happed behind that door, Feldmore didn't return to his bed until very early in the morning. He was limping a little and he grabbed his towel and then headed to the showers. By the time he got back the lights were on and we were all up for first call and throwing on our uniforms to head down for breakfast.

He ducked away from eye contact and when we all compared notes on the way to the messhall, we were all pretty sure he'd been shielding his one side so that we couldn't see the rising black eye. It seemed like the rest of us had gotten off pretty easy both days. Feldmore was a couple of minutes late for breakfast, and he sat down at the end of the table without one word to us. He muttered 'pass the salt' without looking up from his plate.

None of us were very interested in engaging with him and despite his thoughtful silence, he didn't seem interested in talking about what Sarge had 'said' to him. We reported for duty but on the way to the obstacle room. Feldmore was once more singled out and taken away from the group.

We were sent the next morning back to the swamp room. Feldmore sulkily walked over to the group. It was kind of sad, he seemed beaten... well, he was beaten, but I mean spiritually. He was obedient to the enforcement of the group dynamic but it was obvious that his heart wasn't in it at all. He took up my former position at the rear of the troupe and I took point behind Guido. Feldmore followed dispiritedly and we had to stop often as he sunk in the muck. He wasn't trying to survive as part of the group, he had been manacled to it.

When we went near the shore, Feldmore made a break for shore, splashing us all on the way by. Sarge came in, was all snapped to attention in a haphazard, in motion sort of way. He barely gave us a second look and dismissed us, ordering Feldmore to stay behind once more.

Chapter 8: Adventure

"Equipped with his five senses, man explores the universe around him and calls it Science."

-Edwin Powell Hubble

We reentered the swamp room day after day. Each day Feldmore was varying degrees of irascible until, much like being nervous about Sarge, we all just kind of forgot about it. Feldmore was so traumatized and tenderized by whatever happened when Sarge made him train alone, that the rest of us just got used to the fact that Feldmore was pretty sketch.

We all more or less put him out our minds. Our bunks were divided up into three rooms. There were two sets of bunkbeds in the larger of the two room and then a smaller room with a bunkbed and a lone, freak cot. I shared my room with Azain who had the bunk over me, and Midge, who had the other top bunk while Guido used the other bottom bunk. Our rooms all opened up onto each others, but I became closest with the people in my room, we whispered together after lights out.

Originally Reid had shared the little room with Feldmore but after several tearful meetings with Captain Wood she had been given permission to pull her cot into the room I was in and she became part of our 'group'. Feldmore was left to himself in the freak little room that always seemed to be shadowed.

Over time, Feldmore became more helpful to the group, it wasn't as though he was friendly, he was just useful. It helped that he was familiar too, but anytime he walked in and we were chatting and laughing, the sounds would die in our throats. We weren't talking about him, but it looked like we were because none of us ever seemed to have anything to say when he was around. He was fundamentally a betrayer, someone who refused to be absorbed into the group dynamic and so was by definition, 'Other'.

As we became more competent we also started to get the occassional afternoon of leave and we began to explore the space station. Usually it was the five of us, Guido, Azain, Reid and Niblet.

The area with the small barracks and training rooms was cordoned off from the rest of the station mostly by being labelled with a blue arrow representing the GAF. The GAF wing was a pod that was surgically attached to the rest of the station, but in an emergency like a breach in the hull of the main part of the station, the GAF wing was designed to be a survival pod for the entire population of the station until the damage could be repaired. In theory it was also possible to jettison the GAF wing but it was unclear of what purpose this would serve as it wasn't equipped to go into HyperDrive. If it was attacked or stuck in a meteor storm it was unlikely it would get very far. It was probably not equipped with HyperDrive because there wasn't anyone around to attack it. In theory it was possible that brigands or pirates might attack it but there was little of value and it had enough fire power to blow anything but an Armada out of the sky.

The medical ward was at the very end of the blue arrow before you walked through a dual layered steel door that could be turned to an airlock seal with the flip of a switch behind a glass panel. We walked by Dr. Johnson and Sarah who were hanging out by the front desk. I think they were flirting. I blushed and fought down a surge of jealousy. That was a stupid and self indulgent way to think after managing to preserve our friendship after our intimacies. It was the first time in a relationship that I had managed to do that and I was absurdly proud of it. He smiled invisibly at me and gave a wave, I returned each and ran to catchup with my friends.

We were friends, and it was exciting for me because I knew that Reid was going to officer's school as well so it was possible that we might even be sent to the same school.

We wandered around the station, feeling what it was to be part of a larger group. For me, it was a brand new experience. I was used to being a mouse, creeping around and trying to be unobtrusive, and largely succeeding. Now when we walked by, most people looked at us as we passed. It wasn't a big deal, just the natural curiousity any human or most aliens had for anything moving and larger than them.

We were found stores and looked at things from across the galaxy that most of us couldn't afford with our limited credits. Then we rediscovered our old friend and something a bit more affordable: the bar.

On the surface of Dalton, liquor was a controlled substance that was monitored closely. It was also of poor quality and had a tendency to make people who drank more than a small glass of it exceedingly ill. I had had wine and champagne with Stephen, but that had been different, somehow... purposeful yet sterile, and of course, occluded with Dr. Johnson's twin powers of hypnosis and drugging through his stimulated skin proteins.

During the wet t-shirt contest I had been on the stage and I hadn't had anytime to appreciate the fact that this was a place where people, people meaning 'me', could drink. Drinking felt illicit and drinking with boys made me feel very galactic. We didn't have a lot of chances to go off to the bar but we did it every chance that we could manage.

Most of the drinks were out of our price range but beer was cheap. It was cheap across most of the GAGA, but I would discover that later on. It was watery and tasted a bit like soap, but you could drink it and be social and get a buzz from it.

Mostly I was enjoying people watching. I had never seen

people outside of my immediate social strata or outside of a highschool auditorium. I had certainly never had an opportunity to see aliens as well as humans from across the GAGA all co-existing in one small space.

I could sit and nurse one of the soapy, urine coloured beer and watch the lights and the fake smoke billowing around the room and dreamily listen to the piped in music or to the live music if they had a group. I let my eyes unfocus and take in the room.

That was how I first met Howard Donovan.

He was sitting in a corner that should have been darkened, but a rogue yellow spotlight had been left on and so his perch was illuminated and my gaze fell on him. He wasn't like the other people in the bar. Physically there was little to set him apart. A short, dark haired man, his hair curled and seemed to gleam as though shellacked. He nursed one of the electronic cigarettes favoured by bar flies. His lips were full and pouty and his body was slender and whip-like but also entirely relaxed. It wasn't his physical appearance that drew me to him, it was the way he gleamed.

He seemed cleaner than everyone else in the bar, shiny and, just different. He was the first celebrity that I had ever seen in real life. He would not be the last but I began with Howard Donovan. He was the head of Donovan Aeronautics and the inventor of the Jump Drive, but what I knew the most about were his biting soundbites that he would chirp out at new reporters or at celebrities. Howard Donovan was scathing and hilarious and I couldn't believe how much he looked the same in real life as he did on the holos. He was the father of Dominic Donovan and had been repeatedly cited as a mentor to Verily Wrought himself.

It was like a dream to see him in person, the man who had raised one of the greatest pop singers of all time, THE Dominic Donovan, the man who had been more of a father to Verily than Victorinus had ever been. The man who had been voted 3052's Sharpest Dressed and Sharpest Tongued Man of the Year, sitting in the corner with his cigarette, in orbit around Dalton.

Nobody seemed to have noticed him except for me. There was a live performance on. It was a girl named Shelka who wasn't wearing much in the way of clothes and most of the bar's patrons were utterly consumed by watching her gyrations on the stage. Howard Donovan wasn't watching Shelka, he was people watching. His gaze wandered to meet mine and he smiled and waved me over to where he was sitting.

I tried not to react to his invitation, I was worried that Azain and Guido would insert themselves and I wanted to get up close to Donovan. I wanted to get inside his aura and see if it felt the same up close as it did from across the bar, see if it felt better. I left my cheap beer at the table and walked away, Guido briefly glanced over but he was preoccupied and I walked over to where Howard Donovan sat in a meandering path. A part of me was afraid I was dreaming as Shelka belted out the lyrics for a song that I was certain I had heard Dominic Donovan sing first, and much, much better.

First you're going to be my lover

Cuz that'll make us better friends.

Feel my breath against your neck

Hold me tight baby

It's the Galactic Underworld

There's always sunlight in the...

Night of the Galactic Underworld

Where the suns are only stars

Rest in my arms in the darkness

That's the only sun in the land of death

It *was* a Dominic Donovan song, I recognized the chorus despite Shelka's very enthusiastic changes to the dark and sultry tones that Dominic sang in his clear tenor with a deliberate catch in his crooning that made every girl I had ever heard hear it swoon a little. In fact, I recalled hearing it play at Stephen's while we made love. The galaxy isn't as big of a place as you might think and these themes seem to replay and replay.

Howard Donovan smiled at me and pushed out a tall chair for me with his foot. He was nearly finished something that looked like scotch and he was trying to catch the eye of the waitress by waving the glass in circles in the air.

"She's really dreadful," he said, at first I thought he meant the waitress but then I noticed that he gestured to the stage.

"Your son wrote this song."

"Yes, he did... but he didn't write it quite like this, did he?" He was laughing and didn't seem offended. Shelka looked like she was attempting some variation of intercourse with the stage to the general good humour of the majority of the bar goers.

I smiled and took the chair he offered but I didn't know what to say about the song. I wanted him to keep talking, it was a window into his world, into his son's world and it was so different from anything I had ever seen.

I had never known anyone who ever created anything before. I was the only one I knew who kept a journal, wrote things down or drew pictures. I had never met anyone even like Shelka who could be... uninhibted in front of a crowd like this. Whatever else there was to say about her singing, she was certainly born to be the center of attention and a performer of some sort.

The waitress came over at last. I noticed that she was walking quickly to Howard Donovan and knew from my own experiences that the staff at Up Station Bar never hurried for anyone. She smiled at him, trying her best to be charming and cheerful despite the dark circles under her eyes and harried expression.

"Another one of these, and whatever the lady wants."

I stared at him dumbly and then realized that he was talking about me. I was speechless and didn't know what to say. It seemed somehow inappropriate to order another beer, and besides, I had left most of my beer over at my other table... I didn't want to waste that drink and start another one... I must have looked like a landed fish.

"She'll have a cider, something nice, maybe peach if you have it," Howard Donovan decided on my behalf.

The waitress smiled at me a tad uncertainly and went to take the used glass of scotch. Donovan lifted it deftly up and away from her grasp in one smooth motion. "I'll just hold onto this until you get back."

He winked at me after she left. "It's soothing for me to have something to hold."

"I'm Sasha Wheaton," I blurted.

He smiled an inscrutable, cockeyed smile. "You sure are, sweetheart, aren'tcha? I'm Howard Donovan, and it's a pleasure to make your acquaintance." He reached out a hand and I held out mine to be shook but then he flipped it and kissed the back of my hand. I felt electric.

"This place has a decided lack of friendly faces in it," he added, returning my hand to me.

"It does? Is it less friendly here than in other parts of the galaxy?"

"Oh, yes, resource planets tend to breed 'em surly. Are you from Dalton?"

"Yes, but I'll be leaving soon. I'm going to Easty-Westy as soon as basic training is over."

"Joined the GAF, did you?"

His eyes were canny and I could see that he was drawing all sorts of conclusions about me but I didn't have the first idea of what any of them might be. I wasn't even really sure why he was talking to me except that there didn't seem to be anyone else around and he was bored. In most of the pictures I had seen of him he usually had at least one buxom woman hanging off his arm and often many more.

I remembered a kerfuffle he had caused by his insistence on calling his companions, 'floozies'. He had refused to mend his ways no matter how politically incorrect his phrasing was and had alternately laughed and verbosely derided anyone who spoke against it.

He had said: "Freedom of speech even includes jerks like me. I've got every right to call her a floozy and she has every right to be a floozy, ain't no one going to start telling me my lifestyle is wrong at this late stage of the game."

And here was the quotable, floozy-endorsing man in front of me. I blinked, and returned to the conversation. He definitely gleamed close up, even more than he had from afar and he gleamed more the more animated he became.

"Yes, I even paid for officer training," I said this part proudly.

"Well, almost anything will be better for you than being on Dalton, it's a real shit hole of a planet."

"I want to see nice planets," I said wistfully. Our drinks arrived and he relinquished his dry cup for the wet one and a peach coloured drink was put in front of me. I worried about the price of it and then pushed the thought from my mind. It was worth it to dip into what savings I had for the opportunity to drink with Howard Donovan. He lifted his glass in the air, I raised my cider in return.

"Here's to you seeing some nice things in life, sweetheart."

I blushed and clinked my bottle to his glass. It was the weirdest thing, when I met him, I had the feeling that I knew him. I felt safe with him in a way that I hadn't felt safe with any of the other recruits, or certainly how I had felt with Stephen, who I had always felt wrong and, well, alien with. I drank my cider. It would wreck my ability to enjoy the beer, I could tell that at the first sip of fruit and flavour on my tongue.

"How does your family feel about you leaving Dalton?"

"I think it was easier for them than if I had stayed."

He nodded knowingly. "Yes, sometimes family can be that way."

163

"I really liked that song, the one Shelka was singing before... I mean, I liked it when your son sang it."

"Shelka," he said the name dubiously and shook his head with a laugh. "Are you a big fan of my son's?"

"Um, not really. I only know his songs from hearing them around..."

"Well, that's good. I wouldn't want to influence you negatively about him if you were."

"Influence me negatively?"

"Reality can interfere with dreams, do you get what I'm saying?"

"I guess so," I lied. He must have been able to tell I was lying because he chuckled. I blushed harder. The alcohol was turning me pink as well.

"Sasha, where do you want to travel?"

"I don't know, I don't know where all the places to travel to are. I guess I'd like to see some of it so I could decide where I'd like to go to."

We talked for a long while that night. I worried that he would ask me to go back to his room and I worried that he wouldn't ask me to go back to his room. I didn't want him to leave me. It must have been from seeing pictures all the time of him that I felt like I knew him so well. I talked to him like he was my long lost father. I told him about Stephen and I told him about the abortion and about my Dad. I don't know what he thought, he ordered drink after drink and it was three in the morning and they were putting the chairs on the tables so they could sweep the floors before we were finished talking, and even then I wasn't finished talking. It was when I was telling him about my Dad that I put my head on his shoulder. I was very drunk at this point, and he was too.

He put his arm around me and held me and he held me the way I had always wished my real Dad would. His hands didn't wander and his arms were firm and strong despite the masculine smell of scotch on his breath. He didn't try to lift up my shirt but he lowered his head so that he could hear the words I spilled on his chest. I don't know why he listened to me that day. I like to think it was because he felt as connected to me as I did to him.

He did something else that I didn't really notice at the time. He took my arm with my Personal Device on it, and he was fiddling with it. It would be a few days before I found what he had done.

He had left a note on it, and his contact information. His note was short and to the point.

Dear Little Sasha,

This is how you can contact me.

If you ever get into trouble, don't hesitate to call.

Find beautiful places,

Howard.

He walked me back to my room and tucked me under the covers while all my bunkmates were passed out from the cheap watery beer I never could drink again. I didn't realize as I fell into the best sleep I had had since Anastasia was taken that I would be hearing a lot more about that incident the next day.

Chapter 9: Arctic Survival

"When friendship disappears then there is a space left open to that awful lonelines"s of the outside world which is like the cold space between the planets. It is an air in which men perish utterly."
-Hilaire Belloc

I woke up early the next morning because I had to.

Basic training did not stop just because I had had an amazing night with the maker of the Jump Drive. With only three hours sleep and I was quite sure an illicit amount of alcohol still running through my veins, I jumped out of bed and started my morning. Making up my room, showering, dressing and memorizing the meals of the day in case I was called to recite them as still occurred at random times.

We ran to breakfast and I wasn't the only one who was slow moving. Guido and Azain had both been up late as well and I suspected that Guido had found someone to have a bit of fun with from the alternately nervous and happily smug way that he was acting. I knew that I would be thoroughly interrogated at the first chance that everyone had but the morning after being out late was not the time to do so. I found myself almost wishing that they insituted curfews all throughout basic training but was glad that something like a curfew hadn't put an early end to my evening with Howard.

I didn't know then that he had left his contact information on my PD and I felt like a part of me had been awoken that night only to be snuffed out with the dawn. I was tired and miserable and heartsore and sad at the idea that I might never see Howard ever again except in the holos. I felt pathetic that something that likely mattered in absolutely no way to Howard Donovan had made such and impacting difference in my life.

We were informed that we had completed our training in the swamp room and were were to be moved on to the arctic room. We all cheered a little when Sarge announced that we wouldn't be endlessly slogging through the swamp anymore but we exchanged nervous looks when we were told that we were headed for the arctic room.

I had come from an equatorial part of Dalton and even though it was frequently cold, it was never arctic cold. Getting through a swamp was one thing, but dealing with the cold sounded different. It sounded hard.

We were allowed into the equipment room and told to

take whatever we thought would be useful to help us survive several days and nights in subzero temperatures. I found myself wishing that I was built like Feldmore so I could take everything that I thought might be useful, but instead I had to be selective.

Sarge had said several days, so I figured that it would be safe to bet we'd be stuck in there for a week. That turned out to be a good instinct. I picked out the warmest sleeping bag I could get my hands on and a parka. Guido and Midge were arguing over a firestarter kit, seeming to have forgotten that our new laser weapons could be used much more easily than a kit to start a fire. I packed my bag with all the freeze dried rations I could get my hands on and all the Puddin' Hots as well. Those things were awesome in cold weather and could provide a warm 'meal' without even starting a fire.

I got boots and gloves and mittens to go over the gloves. I found a ski mask and a scarf as well. I grabbed a couple of spare sweaters and as many heavy socks as I could find. After that I added tarp, a rope, a small handsaw, an axe and a compass that seemed to mostly work. I put a tin pot and a tin cup and a small piece of metal grating aside and tied them to the outside of my bag. I grabbed handfuls of candles and a package of old fashioned wooden matches. I managed to grab the last emergency battery kit before Guido and then I added my journal and a book I was reading into the pack as well as a couple of pens and pencils.

I was terrified of the cold. I was more prepared for the trip to the 'arctic' than most of the other cadets because of the simple reason that I had read old Earth author Farley Mowatt and had taken his writing seriously. Anastasia and I had played 'arctic' on more than one occasion and I had given what I would take if I could take anything with me quite a bit of serious thought. I had learned a lot of lessons from the books I had read, and one of the things that had stayed with me was: Despair makes the cold colder.

When someone is alone in the cold, it's easy to let your mind wander into some awfully dark places and that's how craziness happens. Things like people stripping off all their clothes and rubbing snow on their naked bodies. People have actually done that and then been discovered, dead and likely in extremely embarrasing positions. Some people say that they don't care after they are dead how they are found, but I've never agreed with that and have always thought that it was important to be found in a somewhat dignified situation if you had to be so inconvenient as to die in the first place.

Some of my terror of facing the cold was rooted in this fear of losing my dignity. What if I went insane? What if I couldn't handle the cold and the dark and Sarge and Stephen had to come in and rescue me while I ranted and railed in the nude and scrubbed myself raw with fistfuls of snow? That would be mortifying.

I had brought the books hoping that by keeping my mind active that I would be able to keep any insanity in me that might be lurking and just waiting to break loose.

I wasn't just worried about my own strength of mind, I was far more worried about how my companions would handle the cold. There was a lot of boasting going on. I overheard snatches of conversation and things like, 'Well, I won't get cold, I'll just keep moving' and other rantings to concern me.

They seemed to think my quiet, purposeful choices of items was as a result of my late night and a hangover rather than legitimate prudence on my part. They seemed to think that we should run in, put up an igloo (which I had read about making but lacked all confidence that I could actually construct one which is why I had brought the tarp), have a snowball fight, make a snowman and then have a big fire to keep us warm while constantly moving until we were allowed to go again. I was worried that when the reality of the cold set in to them that we would have bad cases of case of cabin fever on our hands.

I was especially worried about Feldmore. He had calmed down a lot but he was never going to be exactly 'friendly' and he had a tendency to fall back into 'looking out for number one' at the least sign of stress. Nothing Sarge had done or said had ever completely flushed this habit out of Feldmore and none of us trusted him as far as we could throw the big lug!

Unlike in the swamp room where we had a goal, our only goal in the arctic was to survive it until they opened the door and told us we could leave. This added to the cockiness that everyone was displaying and I felt queasy, although that could have been a hangover.

It was brightly white in the arctic room and not nearly as cold as I had imagined it would be, it was also light out. The holographic sky was unnaturally blue and our breath hung in clouds in the air. When Sarge yelled at us to fall in it looked like he was blowing smoke at us. The sun was low in the sky, my compass said it was setting in the north. There were no trees that I could see in our immediate vicinity and I worried about how I would set up my tarp without anything to tie the rope to.

Everyone was in high spirits, except for me. I couldn't wait for Sarge to stop going over the same information we had already been told once already. Finally we returned his salute and he left the room. The door closed behind him and then, unlike the constantly visible door in the swamp room, this door melted into nothing and appeared seamless from a snowdrift. I peeked at my compass again. The door was the furthest east you could go in this room. That was at least, one point of reference.

A cold wind was blowing from the north and the sun was setting. I wondered what time of year it was supposed to be in the arctic we were in and decided from the fact that there had been a sunrise that it must be late fall or early spring, The sun sank as I watched it.

The snow was powdery and dry and stung our faces in the frigid wind. There was no way that anyone could build an igloo out of that type of snow. My plan for a small tarp shelter wasn't any good either though, not without some sort of tree or

172

something to put it up against. Midge had grabbed a pup tent which surprised me, I hadn't known that there were any available and with all the talk about igloos I was impressed that anyone had thought to expend the energy and space for a back up plan.

It was a tiny little tent, two smaller people could fit in it if they didn't mind snuggling up to each other. My tarp was a bit larger than the tent and so Midge offered to let me use the back tentpoles to use as an anchor point for my tarp. I realized another gross error in equipment that I had made: no shovel.

The powdery snow wasn't accepting of the tent pegs and when I used the back of my axe to try to pound it into the deeper snow that might offer some resistance we lost all but the top five inches of the tent poles. Feldmore had brought a shovel and offered to help us shovel a spot in exchange for a place in the tent or under the top. The wind was rising along with the setting sun and the air was getting colder and harder to breathe by the second. I put on my ski mask and all the other winter clothing I had and helped scrape the snow away with my tin pot.

Midge and I agreed to share the tent and I sacrificed my tarp to Feldmore who argued against the others who wanted to share the tarp with him. I told him that he was stupid not to share it with as many people as he could fit in there since the body heat would only help. Midge was the only one who had gott a tent. It seemed that there had only been one in the equipment room. We scraped a circle free of the top layers of snow and were able to find some ice to pound the tent poles into. The tent was blowing up in the wind and after it was assembled someone had to hold onto it or it would blow across the snowdrifts until we caught it again.

Feldmore agreed to share the tarp with Azain and Adonna but rejected Guido until Guido managed to convince him with a combination of complaining and making himself irrefutably useful. It was going to be tight for all four of them to fit in the tarp and Rich and Felger were still left out in the cold. Rich had taken another tarp but had failed to check it for size and had also forgotten to get rope so it was pretty much just a six by six rectangle. The two of them decided that they would plant themselves on the south side of the tent after attempting for about an hour to make the snow into some sort of shelter. It didn't work at all, it just blew in their faces in those strong, cold northern gusts. Rich was happy to share what little there was of his tarp, he didn't like the idea of being alone in the dark and the cold and was grateful that there were two odd men out. They decided to put the tarp under them and zip their sleeping bags into one sleeping bag to conserve their body heat.

I didn't really know what to do. In theory, this training exercise was just about survival and they weren't looking at us for teamwork or group effort or anything else, but in practice I knew that we all had our weaknesses. We were stronger as a group, even here and even with the poor planning of so many members of the group, we would still do better to pool our resources. Nevertheless, I had the niggling worry in the back of my mind that things were different in the cold and that it wasn't safe to trust them, that the cold drove people to do things they wouldn't do under any other circumstances.

So that first night, I didn't say that I thought it might be a good idea if we all rotate our sleeping arrangements. I didn't want to sleep outside in the cold either, that was why I had picked the tarp... it wasn't a fair trade for me at all. On the other hand, if it weren't for Midge's tent, my tarp would have been just a bigger version of what Rich and Felger were sleeping in...

I was tired from my late night with Howard and I decided not to think any more about it. Midge had brought a rechargeable lantern and she left it on so we could arrange our bed and get ready for the long night. I was happy to make it an early night, I hadn't gotten a lot of sleep before.

I woke up feeling panicked in the dark and the cold. The lantern had died while we had slept and the cold felt like a living, oppressive being in the dark with us, a being that was sitting on my chest and that made breathing next to impossible. I found the candles with the light of my PD and lit one, almost immediately the sensation of being smothered left me but I was panting for breathe from the panic of it. Midge was still asleep. My PD said it was five in the morning.

The PDs were a life saver for those ten days. They are recharged off of our own bio energy so they are almost always fully charged after some sleep and they are kept warm by their nature of being strapped to your forearm constantly. They had tracking chips in them so they are literally a lifeline if you get lost and they read your biometrics and log them into your GAGA account daily. Now that I was a GAF member, they were read by the GAF rather than the GAGA and Sarge or Stephen could pick them out and have a look at them anytime they wanted if they were unsure of your health and well-being. This also essentially meant that none of us were ever really in any danger during training barring some horrible chain of events.

If our body temperature went too low or we went into shock we were unlikely to wake up dead, we were much more likely to wake up looking at Dr. Johnson and wrapped in warm blankets in the infirmary. We would also have a note put into our file and another count against us in the GAF which could make where we would ultimately be placed closer to canon fodder. I knew that they would know about my panic attack when I woke up and how quickly I had been able to recover from it. They would also know if I woke up with panic attacks in arctic conditions habitually or if this was a matter of my having slightly poor adjusting capabilities.

My hands were cold from rumaging through my bag and finding the candle and the matches. I wondered how any of us were going to light a fire and I hoped that a few days was all that we would be here but I doubted it was. I was thirsty but the water that I had brought was frozen. I grabbed a glove full of the powdery snow from outside and tried to eat it but it made me feel somehow drier than before and a lot colder. I warmed my breath with the candle and the sieve against the cold that my ski mask provided. It was an imperfect system as the mouth of my ski mask rapidly grew moist and smelled stale.

I needed to brush my teeth and wash up a bit but I didn't see anyway that that was going to happen. I tried to write in my journal but the ink in the pen had frozen and then I found how quickly my fingers froze up when I tried to write with the pencils.

I also realized that I had forgotten to bring my pencil sharpener. It was getting close to six and the others began to stir out of habit. We didn't have anything to do here.

I found myself wishing that we had some sort of mission, something to find, somewhere to go, just so that we had a focus for the day. I felt completley decontextualized by both the sudden change in locus and by not being told what was expected of us. There was always a goal, and all we had to do was find a way to achieve that goal and then we could for lunch, maybe go to the bar after. Having a mission seemed like a reasonable request.

I would have gone out and gathered fuel for a fire, but I had seen in the light that there wasn't anything anywhere near us that would burn. It was an endless field of powdery snow. The wind was blowing even more fiercely than it had the night before, the sides of the tent were bowed and rippled with its force. I longed to have something to do. I heard Feldmore going through his pack and a mild;y curse under his breath. It seemed I wasn't the only one who felt woefully unprepared now that we were faced with winter.

Midge woke up and I was glad for her company. I shared some of my dehydrated food with her and she revealed her plan of having brought beverages that were spiked with a bit of alcohol. I wouldn't have thought that was a good idea if I had been anywhere warm, but it was a brilliant idea and I was so happy to have something wet on my lips, even though there were ice chips throughout the bottle, it was much better than nothing or the dry snow. The wind and the cold had sucked out all my moisture in the night and my lips were parched and chapped. Midge gave me a chocolate bar and we each ate ours, trying to muffle the sound of the wrappers and giggling with nervousness that the sound would attract the others with whom we might have to share her precious stash of sugar.

It cheered me up to have someone to talk to and we decided that we would hunker in the pup tent and not bother trying to find any fuel for a fire. Rich put his head in the tent and asked us if either of us had anything to start a fire with and I laughed and asked him how we could possibly do that, especially in a tent. Midge giggled when he left and we started to laugh, even though we knew he could hear us laughing at him. I don't know why either of us were laughing, I was worried that I was already starting to lose it.

The sun came up a little that day, but it was barely even there and I suspected that the sunny day we had arrived on the day before had been engineered to be more pleasant just so that they could put us in here without us all just making a bolt for the door and freedom. Northern lights played across the sky, singing an eerie song that sounded to me like the sound of water screaming as it froze.

The lights were bright enough to see the snow drifts. Meteors scored the sky above us. I thought of putting my head on Howard's shoulder and how he had held my head in his hand and hadn't even tried to put his hand on my thigh. He could have, I wouldn't have stopped him. I expected him too but I was so happy that he hadn't. I thought of peach cider and the lyrics to Dominic Donovan's song.

It's the Galactic Underworld

It's always sunlight in the...

Night of the Galactic Underworld

Where the suns are only stars

Rest in my arms in the darkness

That's the only sun in the land of death

I found some of Dominic's music on my PD and played it quietly. Midge hummed along, she was a bigger fan than myself and seemed to know all his melodies.

I couldn't write and I couldn't even read very well because my fingers froze without the gloves and if I wore the gloves it was hard to hold the book and impossible to turn the pages. Midge and I hid in our joint sleeping bag and ate our food and watched holos on our PDs or listened to music. We watched the news.

That was how I discovered that Howard Donovan and I had been being watched the whole time we had sat together.

This was my first experience with how little privacy anyone of interest in the galaxy ever had. I wasn't interesting, I was completely arbitrary, but because of the images I became so. Me drunkenly collapsing on Howard's expensive suit, his obvious affinity and closeness for me, the hours of conversation (much of it that had been transcribed in case people didn't have time to watch five whole hours of my visit with Howard

Donovan). Every last thing that I had told Howard as my surrogate father was blasted across the galaxy while I sat in the freezing cold eating bits of dehydrated meat substitute. My father's abuse of me, the abortion, everything.

I was thankful that I had kept my mouth closed about Anastasia, even when I was drunk and oddly open to a complete stranger.

The others quickly found out about it, Azain and Guido had known about it before me since Guido had noticed who I had been sitting with that night. He had scanned the news before going to the supply room. It was so humiliating to see my pain play out from a neutral perspective and to hear the commentary and speculation about it that nobody even bothered teasing me. It was just too dreadful to even bother with using it as bait against me.

I watched Dominic Donovan comment on the tape. He laughed and said that he had never met me and had no opinion about anyone his Dad chose to drink with in bars on the opposite end of the galaxy.

Midge looked at me with large eyes. She seemed to think that anyone who was on the news was something bigger than life. I guessed that I had thought the same thing and might have acted the same way if it had been she or one of the other on that tape instead of myself. As the days passed and it seemed to us all that only coldness and darkness had ever been or ever could be, the brief scandal was replaced with other scandals and even I ceased to care that my most treasured moments and feelings of safety had been smeared all over the GAGA for people to speculate on.

The arctic training exercise went from a feeling of quiet despair to suddenly very loud in a hurry.

Chapter 10: Monsters

"It is conventional to call 'monster' any blending of dissonant elements. I call, 'monster' every original inexhaustible beauty."

-Alfred Jarry

If it wasn't for our PD's it would have been nearly impossible to know how many days had passed. We were all sleeping a lot, all except for Feldmore and Guido who had taken to roaming about under the northern lights, searching for food to hunt or fuel to burn. In theory we could use our weapons to heat up rocks hot enough to cook a meal on or heat up a small area, but there was so much snow that we hadn't even found rocks. I had discovered that if I set my laser setting to low and shot at my tin pot that it would cook the contents. It was also damaging the pot and every time I 'cooked' something in it I wondered if this would be its last time. I mostly used it to melt the powdery snow. We were all short on water, the small amounts we had all brought had frozen solid in the minus forty and colder weather. We had all resorted to putting the icy bottles in our bedrolls to melt.

A few of the others had tin pots and we all used them for the snow. We were always thirsty now and every drop of moisture was coveted as the cold leached out our water as well as our warmth. Feldmore and Guido were concerning us all as they would come back from their explorations covered in snow and freezing. Azain said that they were both soaked through all their layers of clothing and none of us asked them about frostbite.

Rich did come down with frostbite. He had fallen asleep with his nose and the fingers of his left hand exposed and the tarp had blown off of him. I took him into my and Midges pup tent and had a look at it in the wavering candlelight.

"How does it look, Doc?"

I didn't say anything but continued my inspection. He was trying to be brave but I could see that it had frozen fairly deep. I would have to file a report about it on my PD to Doctor Johnson. I had grabbed my medical kit at the last moment and I at least had sterile Burnagohz strips to cover it but I knew that if he continued to be exposed to the cold that the frostbite would spread even further.

"You're going to have to sleep in here tonight, you can't be exposed to more wind and it's too cold even in here for you."

I packed up my supplies and started to file my report.

"You can't sleep out there, Sasha, it's really cold."

I glared at Rich. I was furious at him and trying to hide it. I didn't want to lose my place in the pup tent, it was possible to seal it up enough to stay marginally warm at least. I don't know why I felt responsible for him, I worried it was the medical training. I unzipped my sleeping bag and took my bag outside with me as well.

"Don't worry about it, Rich," I muttered ungraciously. I went out into the blasting cold air. It was dark. Felger was under the tarp and I told him to gather up Rich's things for him. I put my things beside him and waited for him to sort the things out. I looked up at the creepy light show that was beautiful but utterly unnatural at the same time.

I wished I had a cigarette or something to do to keep me distracted from the cold and also my pissiness at Rich for getting frostbite instead of taking care of himself. I was going to miss Midge and her lantern and her chocolate bars while I was out here. I was also going to miss not having to worry about snuggling without the possibility of Felger thinking that I thought it meant something more.

I moved the things that Felger put outside the tarp into the pup tent and moved my stuff in with him. He was sitting nervously on his side of the tarp. I noticed he had given me the side closest to the tent, which I think was largely the better side as I wouldn't be bound in by the folded over tarp. I put out a silent prayer to Sarge to come and get us soon. Felger helped me to zip our sleeping bags together in silence and then we folded ourselves in out of the wind and then climbed into our sleeping bag and lie awkwardly beside each other.

"Is Rich okay?"

"He has bad frostbite. On his nose and his fingers."

"Is he going to lose them?"

"I don't know, it depends on how long we're stuck here and how deeply they were frozen. All we can do is keep him out of the cold as much as we can, and especially keep him out of the wind."

I turned on my PD and started typing up my report on the vertical keyboard that came up in a holograph along the length of my left forearm. I wondered which side of the tarp Rich had been sleeping on when he had gotten frostbite and figured that statistically it was probably the side I was on since it got a bit more wind than the other side. I put on my ski mask resignedly. It wasn't pleasant to wear and after so many days of my wet breath freezing and thawing on it it didn't smell very nice either.

I didn't want to lose my nose too though. I put my pack up behind me to block out some of the draft, it didn't help very much. I tried to feel sorry for Felger and Rich, stuck out here all this time but I was really feeling much more sorry for myself.

I fell asleep and had a dream that there were lights and voices but when I woke up there was no one there and it was dark and silent. It felt ominous and the wind had died down for once. I decided that I would get up and check on Rich and make sure that his frostbite wasn't starting to smell funky or anything. I brought a candle with me and lit it as soon as I was in the tent. I could see the top of Midge's head poking out of the green sleeping bag, but no sign of Rich. I felt around the sleeping bag and couldn't find him in it.

"Sasha? What's happening?"

"Midge, did you see where Rich went?"

"He's not here?" She asked groggily.

"No, he isn't..." I felt panicked. Where had he gone? Had he decided to head off and rub snow on his naked body? Had the insanity of the dark and cold taken him?

I woke up Guido to ask if he had seen Rich. He hadn't but he put on his boots and started looking around in case he could scout out some sign of where he had gone. Feldmore and the other woke up as well and Midge and Felger came into the large tarp to find out what was happening. I noticed that the message light on my PD was glowing and I tapped it to see what it was.

"Uh, guys, it's okay, I got a message from Sarge, Rich was extracted due to medical danger. He's alright."

"They came in and took him while we were sleeping?"

"Were we all sleeping at once?"

"That's kind of creepy that they came in and took one of us right out of our sleeping bags and none of us woke up or noticed. Maybe someone should be keeping watch."

I felt goosebumps rise on my arms. They were right, it was creepy that they had done a full extraction without waking up a single one of us. I had had a vague impression that I had dismissed as a dream and that was it.

"I think we need to start posting a guard."

"Well, it doesn't really matter, I mean, they took him away for his own good, what are we going to do, stop the Sarge from doing whatever he wants? I don't think so," Azain said nervously, his voice high at the idea of defying Sarge.

"I don't mean because of Rich, I mean because anyone or anything could walk into our camp and do anything to us and it would be awhile before we even realized that we were in trouble."

"Yes, but we're all alone in here," Midge pointed out.

"How do we know we're all alone in here?" Guido asked, his dark eyes were darker with concern.

"We were all alone in the swamp," She insisted.

"No, we weren't, there were all the bugs."

"Bugs that they had to bring in especially for the purpose of making it more realistic." I said, voicing my thoughts out loud.

"There were leeches too," Azaine noted.

"...and they wanted to make it more realistic so that we would get a closer experience to an actual 'on the ground' situation," said Adonna looking growingly concerned.

"But things like polar bears and wolves are what make it more realistic where we are now," I pointed out.

"Wouldnt' we have heard something if there were big wild animals in here, these rooms usually aren't that big."

"But the winds been blowing all this time, Feldmore, today is the first time it's been this quiet."

We were all only arguing now because none of us wanted to lose out on our sleep but there was no arguing what our situation was. There could be anything out there and if there wasn't now, they could decide to introduce a predator or even a combat situation to see how we would handle it. Being told that we had no mission had made us all complacent, as it had no doubt been intended to do.

"Let's make the tent the watch station, that way whoever is guarding can sit up and have a light so that they are less likely to fall asleep."

Midge looked at me angrily for suggesting her tent as the thoroughfare. "I'm sorry, Midge, but we need to do this, and we are supposed to be a group."

I hoped that she wouldn't make this difficult and she was rarely very willful or opinionated. I was relieved when she sighed. "Alright, we can use my tent. But I'm not leaving it so everyone will have to put up with me in there when you're guarding."

By my count we had been in the arctic for five days so far. We each took six hour shifts on guard duty and there were enough of us that it didn't cut into any of our sleep. I slept better knowing that someone was watching out for me while I was resting, but I missed my place in the tent. We started having a rotational sleeping system where we would just take the place of whoever was coming next in the roster, everyone except Midge, who sat like a little queen in her tent. She also was in charge of making sure that someone was always taking their shift and making the shift schedule to begin with. She seemed to be enjoying herself.

I wasn't on guard duty when it happend. I was sound asleep in the large tent, when I woke up to the sounds of something large and ferocious. Adonna had been on duty and she screamed as soon as she heard the heavy, padding footfalls headed towards the camp. The scream seemed to have instigated the animal to attack but at least we had a moment's warning. My pack was right above my head. I grabbed my gun and put on my boots.

It was already chaos and giant paws were stomping in the tarp over top and pulling the tent over with it.

My first thought was to get free of the tarp that had suddenly become a danger. Someone was shooting laser fire and I ducked behind what remained of the tent to try to avoid the wild firing. The bear was bigger than I had ever pictured such an animal to be and was roaring and and stamping. He had part of the tarp rapped around one of his massive clawed paws and I put my pack on my back and got further away from the tent. I sunk into the snow as I got a small distance away. Someone was still firing, I could see from here that there were a couple of people firing.

One of the bolts zipped by me. I checked out the situation as best as I could with my scope and decided that there wasn't anything I could do without adding to the chaos. I tried to hoof it a bit further away still. I remembered reading about the viciousness of polar bears, their excellent sense of smell and their tendency to hunt humans or cause them mischief just for the fun of it.

I kept going. I heard the screams and I saw the laser fire pierce the sky. I kept going under the song of the northern lights and into the darkness.

I was lost for two days in the snow and Iwoke up in the infirmary in much the same way I'm sure that Rich woke up.

Stephen was looking down at me and he was concerned but he smiled at me, even though the worry didn't leave his eyes. The incident with the polar bear had been a rout it turned out.

Feldmore had a broken leg and someone had shot Guido in the shoulder. Midge had to be rescued from the tent after it had been wrapped around her and she had been sat on by the bear for about fifteen minutes while he ate Felger's backpack and the jerky that he had been saving in it.

I had wandered out into the arctic wasteland a lot further than any of us had realized we could go in that space. Apparently it was a very large holo-chamber. They had to send a team to extricate me when my PD showed my vital systems slip into shock. I was happily lying in the snow.

I didn't ask them if I was wearing my clothes when they found me, I was scared of what the answer might be.

I had had some frostbite on my toes and feet and some on my little fingers as well but it was readily healed up by Stephen. I never saw the full extent of the damage, thankfully. I was soon released back to our dorm where we greeted each other with mutual shame.

Chapter 11: The Desert

"I had to live in the desert before I could understand the full value of grass in a green ditch."

-Ella Maillart

We weren't given long to mope, or to heal. Modern medicine can heal you up pretty quick and Sarge was far from sympathetic about the debacle in the arctic. He mocked us in the morning, he told humilitating anecdotes to the other officers every chance he could in a loud voice to make sure that we didn't get the impression that our shame was anything less than public. We were only given a few days but it was long enough for us to get the gist of how thoroughly the GAF could mock and deride its members, and also long enough for me to find out another thing or two about my own earlier humiliation with Howard Donovan and my drunken confessions of being molested by my father.

Stephen took me aside before our next mission and advised me of a few things. The first thing that I was told was that due to the publicity and a general consensus that 'such things ought not to be allowed', there had been an investigation opened into my father's abuse of me. I was told that I would be asked to speak to some police from Dalton before being sent on to Easty-Westy and stronly encouraged to tell the truth to them about anything inapporpriate that may have occurred. It was an unsettling conversation to have with Stephen but I was glad to hear about the investigation from him rather than from one of the other cadets or worse yet, from Sarge.

The other piece of information embarrased me more than anything else that I had heard so far, even more than Sarge's impression that he did of me wandering in the snow and begging him to come and rescue me... that was pretty embarrasing.

What embarrassed me was finding out that Howard Donovan had been at the wet t-shirt contest and had watched me in it. There was footage of the whole thing, he had moved tables to get a better look. I hoped that it was Midge or Adonna that he was looking at, but of course everyone believed it was me, including Stephen who seemed wounded by the entire scene.

It occurred to me that I had done something to him far worse than what I had imagined Sarah to have done and I was grateful that he was still kind to me after everything. We weren't seeing each other when I had 'canoodled' with Howard Donovan, but the whole thing was so terribly public it had to sting a great deal.

We were soon deployed again, this time to the desert, and this time, we had a mission. We had to retrieve a satellite component that had fallen out of orbit and onto a hostile 'planet' and then return with with it to co-ordinates we were given. We were given access to the equipment room and this time, I did not feel like I had any sort of idea of what to bring or what strategy to use.

I didn't have any context for the desert, and at least with the arctic I had read about it so I had some practical warnings even though I had completely lost it during the practical application of those lessons. All I knew for sure was that I would need a lot of water, and a hat, and the lightest clothes that I could find. Guido warned me in the supply room to take a blanket as well and told me that it could get below zero at night. Midge had made a bee-line for the tent and only the small tarp was remaining so I grabbed that before anyone else could.

Everyone was cranky from healing up from their injuries and from the general and specific humiliations we had suffered. It had driven us apart as a team rather than pulling us together. I was happy that we would soon be finished general training, I was getting tired of them all and wanted to see someone new, someone who hadn't witnessed our spectacle of defeat.

We were dropped in the desert without so much as another word from Sarge. I think he was telling the truth when he said that he was disgusted with the lot of us. The door slid shut and the exit sign disappeared. We all shifted on our feet, avoiding making eye contact with each other. I had a compass and I took out my copy of the map and co-ordinates we had been given and sat down on the hot sand to see what I could figure out. As soon as I took out my compass I could see that we were being played with again. The needle was spinning wildly.

Guido came over and looked at it, my expression must have been agog. He sighed.

"There must be a chunk of magnetic rock somewhere around here."

The others came and looked at my compass. Then one by one we tried to find the compass function on our Personal Devices only to find that not a single one of them worked. There was some sort of magnet in here alright, and it was a powerful one if it could get past the shielding on a PD to knock it out.

"Well, this is just stupid," Azain kicked the sand.

I looked around. There were sand dunes, and more dunes, I stood on my tip toes and peered around. I saw a flash of something, something green and then it was gone.

"I saw something, over there," I pointed.

"If we head out without any way of finding our way back we could get lost in the dunes. We could suck this one even worse than last time."

Adonna was very irritated, it was her scream to warn us about the bear that Sarge mimicked for her many times. He did a very pretty job of it and kicked one heel up behind him when he did it.

"I don't want to do this. This is crap," Rich opined. None of us had recovered our spirits since our grand failure. Rich was right, it was crap to put us out here and expect us to find something that we couldn't possibly know the whereabouts of without any sort of compass. He was right, but it was also something that would happen in a real mission and that was the point of training. They didn't really think that we would succeed with amazing luck and vigour, but the way we failed would tell them about us and we had signed a contract agreeing to play this game with them. It was their game and their rules and since they would pull us out if we actually got too stuck- there wasn't any reason not to play.

"I saw something green over there, at the very least, we should try to do something. I don't want to hear about how we are 'pathetic, lazy maggots huddling for warmth' when we are through with this one. I'd rather run around in all directions than have Sarge scream that in my face one more time."

I put my backpack on again and looked around at the others. They shrugged and we all headed out towards the little flash of green that I was pretty certain I had seen.

It was at least as hard to walk in the sand as it had been in the snow. I wondered why they couldn't take the time to give us training in a more average environment only to find out later that on average, most environments were adverse. I was hot, very hot. I wondered how I was going to make it anywhere in here without exhausting my water supply. Wandering and lost in the desert sounded about as fun as being lost in the snow. I wondered if people went crazy in the desert as well.

After walking for several hours I decided that the answer to that must be 'yes'. The sun beat down on us and climbed higher and higher as we walked. I wished we could stop and set up a shelter and I started to stumble under the weight of my pack and from the heat. I tripped and fell and Azain suggested that we stop.

"There's no point in us killing ourselves in the heat, we'd be better off to try to sleep during the day and walk at night."

"It could be harder to spot the component if we are out at night," Midge pointed out.

"It's better than us collapsing before we have a chance

to look for it. Let's set up camp before the sun gets any higher."

We all nodded our exhausted agreement. We had only been out a few hours and we were all exhausted. Setting up the tents was exhausting as well. I was dripping sweat. We set up the tents the same way we had in the arctic, finding a flat place between sand dunes to do so. We decided to keep a lookout right from the start this time, Midge took the first watch and Felger the second.

I was happy to pass out in the relative cool and shelter of the large tarp. The tent wasn't the primo place to be in the desert, it was about five degrees warmer than the big tarp. I fell asleep and woke up to the largest moon I had ever seen staring at me with her pale face. The sounds of the others dismantling the tents had been what had awoken me. I stood up to help them, this was going to take forever if we had to make a fresh camp every morning around dawn and pitch it at dusk.

The cold desert air wasn't nearly as cold as the arctic but the heat from the day and our sweaty skin made the chill extra chill and I was glad that we had decided to keep moving in the night. The cold was still upsetting for me and would continue to be for quite a while.

With each step, I began to doubt myself more. I could see I wasn't alone in this sentiment. The other cadets were glancing sidelong at me. They were thinking the same thing, that this was crazy and that my 'plan' in the arctic was to run around in circles until I collapsed. If it hadn't been a training mission in the arctic, I would be dead now. We could be walking in circles right now for all any of us knew. We tried to keep the moon a little over our right shoulders and I felt like it was still right, but I couldn't prove it, and I worried. It was harder to be sure of the direction after we had woken up and I was disoriented. After awhile a second moon rose, it seemed mocking of us and rode on our left. We all felt like the entire scenario was out to get us and I imagined that was true.

We camped for a second day and then headed out the next morning. We weren't on a timer but we had limited supplies and the longer this went on the more uncomfortable we would all become. We drank our water in small sips and rationed it carefully, there was never enough to drink. I missed the swamp.

On the third morning (which was actually nighttime) we all saw a glimpse of green lit up in the moonlight. It was heartening and the others clapped me on the back and smiled at me again. I thought of their toothy grins and how those teeth would have rent me if I had been wrong... metaphorically, of course.

As we got closer we saw that the green was expanding and was, in fact an oasis. Soon the green defined into dark blue in the light of the second moon. We all picked up our feet at the sight, we were going to be able to camp before dawn on that green! We grinned broadly at each other and drank extra water and trotted on feet that were hot and sweating even in the cold desert air. We were giddy but exhausted when we reached the water. Everyone wanted to dive right in but I remembered in time that as a field doctor it was my job to test the water and make sure it was safe, and not say, a pool of acid or somesuch sitting out in the make-believe desert. I got out the water tester and everyone watched anxiously at my face as I waited for it to read the water.

After fifteen of the longest seconds imagineable a light on it turned green and I grinned at them. Azain didn't give me a chance to tell them it was safe, He tackled me like a maniac, gear and all into the water with a grin and a shout that might have been, 'cannonball!'.

We swam until we were exhausted and had quenched the thirst on our mouths and the thirst on our skins. We had to set up the tents and tarps to prepare as the sun had already risen and was drying the clothes and gear that Azaine had doused in the oasis pool. We slept long that day and woke up to the moons already high in the sky once more.

I got up and went to the pool for a swim. We had forgotten to set a guard last night. I berated myself but I was glad that everyone else was sleeping and stripped down to my underwear for some quiet time under the moon and in the tranquil pool. I had never done such a thing before. I had never been swimming outside in my life. Even though it wasn't really outside, it was impossible to tell that, it was nicer than any outside I had ever been in. The air moved softly and rustled the leaves of the palm trees. It was cold out but the water retained the heat of the day and it was warmer in than out. I played with the reflections of the twin moons on the water as though they were something I could catch on the water. I dove after them when they seemed to slide through my fingers and I felt the sand at the bottom of the shallow pond slide moistly through my fingers.

I found a stone at the bottom of the pond and when I came up for air, I looked at it under the moonlight and was startled to see that it was dark blue and nearly clear, it sparkled magnificently. I put it in the cup of my bra and dived down to see what else hid in the silt and the shadows at the bottom of the pond that was deeper than I was tall but only by a foot or two. I dove down two more times, I didn't find anymore of the stones but I found something else. It felt like a metal handle and it was smooth except for some paint chips that had been taken out of it. I pulled on it but I could only budge it, it was heavy!

After a few more tries to move it I saw that someone was watching me from the shore. I recognized Feldmore and called him over.

"Pssst! Hey! Pssst!" I didn't want to wake everyone up, I don't know why I didn't want to, I didn't want to disturb the moonlight and the water with too much excitement. Having the other cadets around was not unlike being in an unruly litter of puppies.

Feldmore walked over to the edge of the water cautiously. "Wheaton? What are you doing?"

"I found something... in the pool, but it's too heavy for me to lift on my own, could you try to move it with me?"

He was whispering too when he replied, "Alright, what do you think it is?"

He was already removing his clothing and slid into the water in his underwear. "I don't know, I'm hoping, well, I'm hoping it's the satellite component."

I showed him where I had dove down to find it and then dove down again to make sure it was the right place. He went under the water and stayed down long enough for the ripples to fade, he came up a moment later towing the handle. I helped him drag it to shore and we pulled it out of the water to get a look at it.

It was definitely the satellite part that we had been searching for. We shook hands in triumph over it then he shook himself off like an enormous dog and started to gather bits of fallen wood. After watching him for a bit I realized that he was going to start a fire for breakfast. I was stunned, we had never actually managed to make a fire yet. I thought it was an excellent sign for us! Water and fire, what next?

Slowly the others started to wake up. I showed them the satellite and told them about finding it, but I didn't tell them about the stone I had found. I told them how Feldmore had drug it to the surface but Feldmore sat aloofly a ways away by his fire and only grunted when Guido clapped him on the back and told him, 'Hey! Good one!"

We folded up the tarp and sat around Feldmore's fire and talked about how we were going to move the satellite part and more importantly, where the co-ordinates were that we were supposed to take it to for our rendezvous.

"We aren't mind readers! How are we supposed to know where to take the thing?" Midge asked furiously.

"We could just stay here, the rendezvous point is as likely to be here as anywhere else when you think about it rationally," Guido pointed out.

I could see his point rationally, but I somehow doubted that any challenge they thought up would be so convenient as to let us spend a couple of days swimming and resting in the shade while we waited for extraction.

Azain fiddled with his PD angrily and tried to make it work. All of us tried ours again to see if anything had changed. It hadn't.

In the end we decided that the only two choices were to lug the satellite all the way back to the entry point and hope that was the right place, or to stay right here and bet that this was the right place. We decided to stay put at the pool and gamble that they wanted us to stay put since it was better than running all over the desert hoping that we hit on the right choice. I felt niggled at that we were taking the easy way out. I stripped down to my underwear and jumped in the pool and decided it wasn't worth arguing about. We put up the tarps again.

We were extracted three days later by a very angry Sarge who came walking over the sand dunes to yell at us in person. "What the hell do you horses asses think you're doing? Swimming in the middle of the desert? What do you think this is, holidays?"

Most of us had been swimming when he showed up and none of us looked very upbeat. Midge was tanning in her panties and sat up with her hands covering her breasts. I was in the water and chose to stay there, treading water and staring at Sarge as though he were an apparition.

"Why are you all just sitting here and not making your way to the extraction point?"

"We aren't mind readers, Sarge! This whole thing wasn't fair, our PD's and compasses don't work!" Midge was still angry about the whole, 'not mind readers' thing. When she wasn't napping in the sun, swimming, or flirting with Azain to irritate Adonna, it was pretty much all we heard about.

Sarge looked at her. She stood up, one arm on her hip and the other across her breasts. She glared for a few minutes, he seemed unsure for one split second, but it wasn't about our broke PD's that he was unsure about, it was the surprise at being confronted by Midge who had never once confronted him the whole time she had been clothed. He narrowed his eyes at her and walked over to the satellite component. He inspected it for a moment and then bent over and flicked a switch. The component hummed slightly and the lights came back on my PD, I could see its screen staring back at me as I treaded the water.

I struggled out of the water and entered the co-ordinates. Yep, it was just as I had thought, we were nowhere near them. We all wanted to tell Sarge he was being unfair, how were we supposed to know the satellite could somehow augment our PD signals enough for us to be able to use them once it was turned on? None of us had the balls to say anything. It had been so easy just to look at the thing and flick the switch. None of us had even looked at it since we had decided to stay here.

Two total fails in a row. I knew this wasn't going to bode well for any of our future placements. I was lucky, I still had officer school to go to, at least I might have a chance at redeeming myself. We all hung our heads and gathered our gear. We weren't going to hear the end of this.

Chapter 12: Guilt

"No work or love will flourish out of guilt, fear, or hollowness of heart, just as no valid plans for the future can be made by those who have no capacity for living now."

-Alan Watts.

I would be Lieutnenant Wheaton by the end of the year, assuming I didn't do anything horribly wrong and get myself courtmartialed or killed in the meantime. Everything was going very well for me. I had established myself as a leader amongst my troop and on top of that I was not only respected but also liked. I had completed above and beyond field medic doctor and if I wanted to I could continue on and be trained as a full doctor or even a surgeon. I had helped out with some surgeries and I had done very well at them.

The final month of training was a run through of a lot of the things we had learned our first months. We were sent through the swamp room again and aced it- we never were allowed back to arctic or desert training. I could do pushups and could complete the obstacle course without always being the last one to do so. I collected commendations from everyone I could in the forms of letters that I submitted to be added to my permanent record file.

I sent Howard Donovan a message and asked him for one as well, which he sent much to my surprise, along with a brief note wishing me well and expressing congratulations on finishing basic training. I approached Stephen and Sarah who each wrote me one. Sarah was cheerful with me and I could see that for knowing I was leaving in only weeks that she had forgiven me for everything and was more than happy to write something that would help me get off the space station.

Even Sarge wrote me a note that said I was satisfactory in many areas!

Even though I was going on to officer's training with high commendations from almost all the people I had learned from and trained with, I began to feel that something was deeply and seriously wrong with me.

I started to get terrible pains in my chest.

That was the first thing I really noticed, but besides that,

I was increasingly dizzy, distracted and disoriented. I began to have nightmares and then I started to have insomnia as I tried to stay awake so that I wouldn't have more bad dreams. Not sleeping became a habit, and before I knew it it was as though I had forgotten where my 'sleep' button was. I started to feel like a dead-eyed automaton, and then I started to drop the ball in training.

I didn't feel like talking to anyone about the problems that I was having. I didn't want to disappoint them and it felt like if I talked about it, it would validate the nebulous symptoms into a reality and then I would have a problem. It was Feldmore who tracked me down to talk to me.

"Hey! Wheaton!"

I had been sitting at the end of the table in the mess hall. I was by myself and had been working hard on radiating a sort of 'stay away' vibe to get some peace and quiet to myself. Feldmore appeared to be immune.

He climbed over a bench as though it were barely there and then sat astride the bench where I was sitting and put his tray between us. He started to eat even as he started to talk to me. I guess feeding a machine of that size and strength isn't something that can wait, even for an earnest and heartfelt conversation.

"Hi, Feldmore." I said without enthusiasm and pushed

my tray away. I hadn't been hungry before and I didn't want to eat with someone else, the shared communion with another human made me feel inexplicably lonely. Sarge wasn't working very hard to train us now, he seemed to be done with us and we all had a lot more time to ourselves.

"We've all been talking about you lately."

He shoved a third of a loaded baked potato into his mouth and talked around it. It's presence barely seemed to slow him down.

"That's great."

"Yeah, well, not really. We've all decided that you've got a problem and I'm going to talk to you about it."

"I don't have a problem," I advised him, watching in facination. His massive plate load of food was over half gone already. He must have inhaled it.

"You do, and I think I know what it is."

I didn't say anything. I felt sicker than ever. My head

started to pound and I felt like if I could just lay my head down on the table and go to sleep that the majority of my problems would go away.

He ignored my silence and continued in his now usual robustly cheerful obliviousness. "You're depressed. That's all there is to it. You're sad and I think that you need a friend right now that you can talk to and you don't even know it."

"I don't have anything to say."

I was so tired and his concern and his friendship was inexkplicably making me feel like having a good cry.

"Maybe you don't right now, because I kind of caught you off guard, and I get that. No one wants to make you feel like you've done anything wrong just because you got sad. I saw it happen at home with my Mom and my older brother all the time."

"Why were they sad?"

"My Dad was a Large Operator in the uranium mine at mid-equator. The really big one. My Dad always said that they were going to split the planet into pieces because they dug so deep and he was pretty sure it was the mid-equator one that was going to crack that sucker. He came up one time and his meter had gone black all of a sudden like. It turned out there was a leak in the shielding on the machinery he was working on, dosed him and he came home real sick."

"I'm sorry," I said the words but I felt remote from the situation. I had never really thought of Feldmore as coming from a family or of him having lost someone and I didn't feel like I could begin to imagine his father now. I was trying to have empathy but my own emotions were just too fried.

"Yeah, thanks. It was real bad. I mean, really really bad. His guts were fried and he was crapping blood. It was sick. He had nose bleeds and he started coughing up blood. He eyes turned red and they bled a bit sometimes too. He'd wipe the corner of his eye like a guy who was trying to be sneaky and wipe away a tear and it'd come away red. Then he started coughing more, they said he died of bronchitis. That was the official cause of death on the certificate that my Mom brought home from the morgue. Wrought Munitions doesn't pay out casuality benefits to families of worker's who die of bronchitis. Dad didn't even die at work, he died at home in his own bed, it wasn't work related, you get me? Wrought Munitions paid for his funeral and that was it."

"Even though his dosimeter had turned black?"

Feldmore nodded, his eyes were big. He scraped some

gravy off his plate with the side of his finger and licked it off.

"Yep, they said it didn't matter, that it was a safe dose and that he was moved to different equipment immediately after the 'event'. "

"What did you guys do?"

Feldmore shrugged. "Well, we lost our house, we moved to a little apartment and Mom took whatever work she could and my brother and I did any odd jobs we could come across to help out a bit as well."

"Your Mom and your brother had pretty good reasons for getting sad."

"Yeah, there was more too. You see, Dad didn't want to be a Large Operator. He hated that big equipment, in fact, he hated mining, hated the energy sector, hated Wrought Munitions and most of all, he hated Dalton. He wanted to leave Dalton since he was a kid and that was all he had thought of. He was going to join the GAF, it was his life's ambition, but that was before he met Mom. She convinced him to work on Dalton, just for a little bit. That was what he told me on his death bed. He didn't tell me to wreck me, you know? He was pretty confused by that point, the radiation messed with his head pretty good and it was like shit and puke was coming out of his body and words were coming out of his mind. He had the verbal runs. It was like he was trying to pour an entire lifetime of being my dad into the short time he had left."

"Before the 'bronchitis' got him," I said wryly, shaking my head. It was the sort of cost analysis equation that my mother had talked about with me on more than one occasion. She had learned about it from her secretarial duties. She had thought the executives very clever for thinking of all the ways they could save insurance money by blaming colateral damage on a plethora of worker blunders or 'natural' illnesses.

"If he hadn't have been a good guy, he would have just left my mother and joined the GAF. She told him she was pregnant and so he married her. Turned out she was 'mistaken' but she got pregnant with my brother a couple of months later and then I made it a couple of years after that. Suddenly my Dad had to save up for his whole family to go and colonize some place else. He had no choice but to keep punching in that time clock until it finally punched him in."

He had licked all the gravy off of his plate and was regarding the empty plate as though it held all of his woes on it. I offered him my plate silently. He took it gratefully and started eating it with gusto.

"My Mom had the sads way worse then my brother, when I asked her about it, asked her why she couldn't move on with her life, remarry, get happy again, she said it was the guilt and the shame. I missed my Dad a lot, I still do, but I wasn't really old enough to feel bad about the sacrifice he made for us. I knew I wanted off Dalton and when he told me about the GAF I said right away to myself, 'well, that's for me. The GAF's my cup of tea'. I had a goal and just knew that I had to help make ends meet and get enough food and clothes that fit until I was old enough to sign up. But for my mom, she couldn't move on because she had to punish herself."

For the first time since we had started our conversation his eyes fastened on mine. He lost all interest on everything except me and the answer in my eyes. "Now I'm thinking the same thing is true about your sads. Some sort of guilt had crept up on you and you're bound and determined to punish yourself. Well, it's going to work, it seems to me that it's a real easy thing to do. You'll fail at everything now unless you reach into your heart and figure out what's got you in the sads and work it out."

"Did your mom ever work it out?" His gaze dropped from mine and he went back to my plate of food.

"No. She never did, Sasha." Feldmore never used my first name, just like I never used his. His use of it made my throat catch.

"What happened?"

Feldmore had finished my plate. He stood up abruptly.

"I could get the sads myself thinking about it, it's my own shame. She died, she heard I was leaving and she took her own life. She never left a note, she just did it. I'll never really understand why."

He picked up both of our plates and took a deep breath.

"Sorry, it's hard for me to talk about, it's still real fresh, you know? Point is, these things have to be talked about or you act like an asshole who thinks he can take care of himself and nearly gets himself killed in a swamp. Talk to me anytime, Wheaton. Me or any of the others, or anyone you feel OK about talking to. Just talk."

I didn't talk to Feldmore that day or that night, but now that he had brought it to my attention I could see that the others in my troup were watching me and that they were whispering behind their hands. Their smiles to me were nervous, their voices were too kind.

That night while I couldn't sleep on my bunk, I thought about what Feldmore had said to me, about the shame and the guilt that had brought out the sads. I had a lot to feel shameful about.

I started to mentally list them off to myself, counting on my fingers in the dark and listening to the snores of my bunkmates as I did so.

•

> 1. I had lost Anastasia. Just the thought of her made me writhe unhappily on my bed. I had never forgotten about her, surely not, but I had somehow put her out of my mind. Everything had been so busy since I had started basic training... well, everything had been so busy up until real recently.

That was the thing with basic training. It didn't leave you time for the sads, or for guilt, or for even a thought to really cross your mind. It was a different world than the place I had come from and without any context of the past and a physical schedule that left me falling asleep before I hit the pillow each night, all those uncomfortable thoughts hadn't had a chance to surface. That had been convenient and pleasant, until it had stopped.

> 2. I had abandoned my family. Well, sure, they had done things to kind of deserve abandoning. They had abandonded Anastasia to an unknown fate and sundered the whole family, or at least Daddy had. Mom hadn't known about it.

That was part of what had made me so angry with her, I thought, had made me angry with her my whole life, really. She never saw what was in front of her face and a handful of pills kept her floating above anything she could ever possibly feel. She refused to deal with it.

And then it hit me.

I was doing the exact same thing my mother had done with medication but I was using basic training and my new life in the military to hide me from my past and my present. I didn't need to leave the GAF, in fact, I couldn't leave, I was under contract. So why not give my Mom a call and find out if she was alright?

I tried to find empathy for my Mom and was bothered by what I saw. She had lost one daughter already and then, she had lost her husband. It was uncomfortable seeing that, after all, I certainly hadn't been trying to take her husband from her. When I was small all I had wanted was for her to see what was happening and to put a stop to it, and when it had happened again, I had felt the same way. I blamed her for not stopping it. Now there was an investigation, who knew where that could end up for her, nowhere good, that was certain.

She was my Mom, she did have an obligation to protect me, but at the same time, if she didn't protect me, if she didn't stop him, then maybe she couldn't. Maybe in her case wouldn't and couldn't were the same things and that was what had made me feel very free to leave and to not even say goodbye to her.

The thing is though, I couldn't change the way my mother behaved towards me or Anastasia, I could change the way I acted to her. I could show her behavior that wasn't a mirror of her neglect of me.

If I did that, I was a human being. If I just reacted to her the same way she treated me, I was not only the same caliber of person as her and did not have a right to look down on her, I was also hardly more then an animal or an amoeba. I was reacting to stimulii without a single thought.

3. The thing that happened with Daddy.

That was the worst of the shame right there. That was what made me go from feeling uncomfortable with the person I realized I was to having those stabbing pains in my heart. It was the source of the sads more even then losing Anastasia. I forced myself to think about it and try to bring some clarity to my train of thoughts.

What had happened with Daddy, it wasn't my fault. He forced me. I got away from him the first chance I could and I fixed as much of the damage he had done to me as I could possibly fix.

Then it hit me again. One of those heart stabbing realizations that makes you realize without thinking, without

220

feeling, that you are not who you thought you are.

I had 'fixed' the damage. I had gone into the 'doctors' and had the problem taken right out of me so I could go on and do what I wanted with my life and get away from Daddy. Somehow I hadn't thought, even for a moment, that maybe I wasn't alone in my decision and that maybe I didn't even understand the choice that I had made.

I had been convinced that when I realized I was pregnant that it was one of the many children that would never be born because of mutation and flaws, that at best it would be a terrifying monster that would stare at me with blind eyes and if it could, it would scream in pain until it died.

But what if it was a normal, healthy baby?

What if I had killed my son or daughter and never even thought of it afterward except to think of my own minor discomforts from the surgery that had removed them?

Not removed, I realized, killed. Because it had been alive. That was the thing right there. It had been alive and I had killed it and I hadn't even really given it a second thought.

I was a soldier now and soon I would be an officer.

Much of the life I had chosen for myself would lead to be killing or being killed. Once I was an officer, it was likely that I would decide who would be killed and direct others to do the killing for me. How terrifying for everyone around me that the very first kill I ever made was done as thoughtlessly and remorselessly as swatting a fly, from the inside out and without a backward glance.

How was I any different from Daddy? He had a child who had inconvenienced him so he got rid of her. I had a child who inconvenienced me so I got rid of him or her. At least Daddy had let Anastasia live, had raised and provided for her.

I bit the knuckle of my index finger, trying to stifle the sobs that were gripping me, ripping me apart. I cried as quietly as a I could into my pillow but then I threw myself from my bed and ran down the hall to the bathroom.

I let myself cry then. It was the deep wrenching, wailing sobs that are ugly and hurt so bad that you wish more than anything that if there is a god, that he will stop your heart, stop the pain and you will die.

What if the baby I had killed was like 'Stasia? What if she was like me? What if he was like Feldmore? What if they were just themselves and that self would now be forever unknown. I had robbed myself forever from knowing. What arrogance that I thought my life and my future were so important that I could throw that away without a thought.

I had used my Daddy's blood money that he had only had by getting rid of Anastasia, by selling her out, to kill what was in my personal way.

The knowldedge of my crime was so great that it robbed me even of my tears. I sat with my head against the cold tiles and the sadness was gone and all I was then was empty and bereft.

It was then that I fell into a state of utter despair and it was only the fact that I had no choice but to get up and go through training that kept me from just pulling the covers over my head and never getting up again. I wished that there was someone I could talk to about the moral issues that I now had but it turned out that nobody really seemed to see what I had done wrong. I struggled with it, I thought about it all ways and I finally brought up a message to send to my mother.

Dear Mom,

I hesitated for a few minutes before continuing, I wondered if I should address it to my Dad too. Did I want to leave Mom with the pretense that things were anything approaching normal? I thought of Anastasia's warmth in my arms and the sound of her laugh. My jaw clenched at the thought and I raised my chin in defiance. She always allowed herself the luxury of oblivion, why should I grant her the same luxury?

I don't know what Dad told you, but the truth is...

I trailed off again. The truth is... what was the truth? The truth was that I had run away, but the truth was also that I had a good reason to. How much truthfullness and how much was cruelty at this point? What was the point in going over everything?

I deleted what I had typed so far except for 'Dear Mom,'. I looked at the blank screen and felt despair creeping around me with it's long skelatal finers once more. I squared my shoulders and shoved the despair away. I didn't need to be cruel to her, but I would be truthful.

'I had to leave. I've joined the GAF and I've signed on for a five year stint. It's Ok though, I'm ok, Mom. In fact, I'm doing really well here and I'm happy, or at least, I'm learning that I can be happy again.

I looked at the screen again, thinking of my stifled despair and deleted the sentence starting with 'In fact,'.

'I'm as ok as I can be without Anastasia. I miss her every minute of every day. I don't believe what you guys told me, I don't believe that she is dead. I don't think you believe

she is dead either. I think you know a lot of what goes on in the house, far more than you would like. If you didn't know as much as you did you wouldn't have to blot it out with so many pills, would you, Mom?

I'm trying to be truthful without being cruel to you, because I love you and that will never go away. The truth is cruel though, it's cruel because you have never faced what went on under your roof, under daddy's roof. I've done a lot to avoid the truth too, but I know that that's the wrong thing to do. You never meant to teach me that as a lesson, but it's the biggest lesson I ever learned from you, a lesson of negatives, I learned that you made the same mistake as long as I've ever known you, you avoid the truth.

I miss Anastasia and I don't want to work at the nuclear plant. I don't want to live on Dalton and I don't want to live with daddy and I don't want to live with you.

The truth is... Mom, the truth is that I was miserable and Daddy treated me badly and you didn't do anything to protect me. Anastasia protected me and now she's gone. It's wrong that I had to rely on my little sister to protect me from him, you helped him hurt me when you didn't step in to protect me.

I looked at the letter I had written. Why was I even bothering to write a letter to her? I had thought to write to her because everyone wrote to someone, it seemed. I had been thinking that it would be nice to soothe her mind and to make sure that she knew that I was ok. It seemed to be devolving

225

into giving her a piece of my mind.

There wasn't anything Mom or anyone else could do about my decision to join the GAF now. I had been so busy I hadn't had much time to analyze my situation and think about my choice to join up. It had been the only option available to leave Dalton, the only option to get away from Daddy. Would I have made it again?

Even after everything I loved Daddy too. I loved them both, but it was in a weird way, like the way you love a dog, even after it's bitten you. If you couldn't put it down and you had to keep living with it, I guess you'd go on loving it, especially if it was nice most of the time. It's familiar and it's realy hard to find anyone in the whole galaxy who gives a damn about you.

And that... that was why I was glad the GAF was my only option, because even though these people weren't very nice, and most of them bit me a lot, they absolutely gave a damn about me. If anyone was going to bite me, it was going to be them and heaven protect anyone else who tried to get a nip through their jealous line of 'defense'.

That was what I thought before I was sent off to the Officer's Academy. I thought that I had found a group that accepted me regardless of whether or not they actually liked me. They appreciated me for the skills that I had, for my abilities as a leader, someone who was reliable and as a field

226

doctor too. That's what I told myself.

We weren't going to be together after this. I was being shipped off to Easty-Westy, the officer training planet.

This was another thing that I learned in my last week orbiting Dalton: I learned that Sergeant Wommer was a cognizant and human being.

The whole time we were there he was a force in my life that I responded to with yellings of, 'yes, sir', 'no sir', 'absolutely sir' and the ubiquitous, 'right away, sir'. He taught me to yell. Before Sarge, I think I could count how many times I had yelled in my entire life on the fingers of both hands. He had yelled in my face, made me do laps, push ups, sit ups, remake my bed dozens of times, laughed at me, mocked me, derided me and pointed out every last one of my flaws again and again and again. He had cuffed me on the head and put his boot on my back while I did push ups. He had called me flabby and my muscles lost their strength when his head would whip around to look at me.

Staring at the ground I would watch with horror as his large, shiny black boots and perfectly creased pants walked towards me. He would bend down and peer around so that his face was mere millimetres away from my own and then he would bark as often as not, "What are you looking at, cadet?"

"Nothing, sir."

227

"And did I ask you, to look at nothing?"

"No, sir!"

"Well then, if you have enough leisure time to sit around not looking I think you'd best give me fifty laps."

"Yes, sir!" I would yell in his face as loud as I could and salute and bolt off to run lap after lap. I was so happy to be able to get away from him at that point that my feet seemed to fly and I would run around the track for the first several laps before remembering that I had forgotten to count.

Everything with the Sarge was like that. I learned later that that was the sign of a good sergeant. They aren't supposed to be your friend and you aren't supposed to realize anything when they are around except that they are your master and whatever they say goes. It doesn't matter how nonsensical it might seem, they are Sarge and they must be right.

I have never been very rebellious and I have always avoided trouble so this was a fairly easy lesson for me to learn. What was more difficult was dialing it back after we had all graduated from basic training to realize that now Sarge was just another person on the station.

It was exactly as though as mask had dropped from his face and he congratulated us all and shook our hands and... he was smiling. Just like a human being smiles! I watched him in the mess and I realized that he ate food with people who he considered to be his friends and that furthermore, they legitimately liked him in return.

Had he always joked and laughed with them or was this something that he put away while he was doing his training of us. I tried to remember but I honestly couldn't. When I tried, all I could see was his face, nearly as close to mine as a lover's face, his lips snarling, saliva spraying my eyelids and lips. He could have been singing and dancing and I wouldn't have noticed as I was so busy looking at nothing and not looking at nothing. No matter what answer I gave to that question, it was always the wrong one.

We had between a week and two months before we would be shipped out. Those who were not going on to officer academy were being deployed. It gave me the shivers to realize that they would be sent into combat so soon and I was very grateful that I had had the money to buy my way into officer's academy. They could be sent anywhere, into any situation. They could be shot at, they could be lost in space, they could be abducted, they could be exploded... suddenly it occurred to me that I would one day reach the end of training myself and then I too could have any number of dreadful fates in front of me.

I packed my things after the graduation ceremony. We were no longer expected to report for training and until we were told where we were going and when we would all be in the same limbo as I had been when I had first arrived at the space station.

That was the thing with space. Co-ordination was everything. No one was going to send a whole spaceship to pick up one cadet or one soldier just out of basic training. That didn't even begin to make sense. So we would wait.

I knew that I would be sent to Easty-Westy and that was the only thing I was sure of. Guido was going there too but it was a big planet and even though we both kind of hoped we would see each other there it was highly unlikely.

Easty-Westy was where all Officers for the GAF were trained. The entire planet was designated for it and it was close to GAGA and GAF Headquarters in the Telamer star system. I was glad to have some sort of anchor point in my mind for where I was going, but besides the name, Easty-Westy, I knew nothing about the planet and nobody else from Dalton seemed to either.

I was pondering the great uncertainty of it all and folding my socks when Sarge came into the room. He smiled at me.

I was instantly terrified and I could see that my terror amused him. It wasn't particularly sadistic, it was just that he had seen it so often before and could tell that I had fallen for the game the same way that thousands of other recruits had fallen for it. It wasn't a failing on my part, it actually meant that the military system, and I within it, was working.

"Do you mind if I sit down?" He asked and his voice just sounded... normal.

I nodded and then blurted out, "Yes, sir!"

I was horrified I had just nodded my head and I stood staring at him down my nose with my head pulled back and my neck scrunched up, waiting for the hammer to drop. He waved it off.

"At ease, cadet. This is an informal visit. I wanted to talk to you about your prospects."

He pulled the chair over to be close to the bed and sat down with the back of the chair under his chin, facing me. I sat down on the bed cautiously, wondering if this was Okay and what might happen next to me. He laughed a little and smiled in what on any other human being would have been a completely reassuring smile.

"You may not know this Wheaton, but I've been watching you."

"You have?" I couldn't help the stutter in my voice and I began to wonder if he was coming onto me.

"Yes. You have a lot of potential... and I have a suspicion that if you were given your druthers, you would pick an officer's academy that would plunk you down as an aid or a secretary for HQ and that would be the last we would ever see of you. Am I right here?"

"I had never thought of that. I didn't realize that there were different types of schools for officers."

"Oh, yes. They are all very different. It's one of the perks of being a Sarge that I get to give recommendations for all the new recruits and where I think they might best be situated. Did you know that was part of my job?"

"No... I thought your job was... umm, training us."

"That's only a small part of my job. I have to file reports on each of you little buggers at the end of every day to report on everything. Everything I make you do, everything that you do, how you react, when you fart, everything. I make a larger report at the end of each week, an overview at the end of each month and then the last week coming up before graduation I right the big recommendations."

"And they put us wherever you tell them to put us?" I was aghast at the amount of power he had over us all. Things weren't nearly as random as I had thought and I was pretty sure that the Sarge was insane, he had to be. No sane person could possibly spit when he yelled as much as the Sarge could.

"Well, it's not quite as simple as that. Everyone who has an interaction with you while you're in training writes a report on you, or at least they are supposed to, of course things get overlooked from time to time. I can tell you that the guy who ladles porridge in the mess made a report on you every single day that simply said you smiled and said, 'thank you' when he served you breakfast."

I tried to think of who he was talking about and it took me a moment before I could bring the image to mind. I didn't even remember smiling and thanking him. I had done it everyday?

Sarge nodded. "You could see how that sort of information could be valuable, much more valuable than the commendation letters you so carefully collected. Basic training is some of the most stressful time in a recruit's life. We build up a detailed picture of what you're like under pressure by gathering these reports. Someone at HQ has been compiling the reports form your entire class and you will all start to find out where you will be headed out to shortly."

"Why... why are you talking to me?"

His laughter was as barking as his orders and I flinched away from him which made him bark more laughter. "I told you, I've been watching you. You're a good girl and you're also a lazy girl."

My cheeks flushed with embarrassment and he watched me for a minute. I felt like crying, which was stupid because he had said so much worse to me.

"It's true. You're one of the laziest recruits I've ever seen. The only things that saves you is that you are so fundamentally lazy that you get your work done as quickly and efficiently as possible and also that you hate getting into trouble even more than you hate doing stuff."

"I don't really think that's fair, Sir."

"Oh, it's fair. I'm a good judge of recruits and that's why I'm here. Let me ask you something, Wheaton, what did you want to do with your life before you joined the GAF?"

Nobody was technically supposed to point blank ask each other questions about where they came from in the GAF. It wasn't exactly against the rules, but it was considered poor form and so far nobody really had breached that etiquette with me. I understood why as the past came flooding back to me and I mumbled my reply. "I wanted to work with special children, to have a daycare."

He nodded as though this justified everything he had said so far and I was so irritated I had to concentrate to avoid balling my hands up into impotent little fists.

"I've recommended you for BirchBough. I don't know if they will take me up on it for certain, it's a bit of a reach for you and they've gone against my hunches before, but it's what I'm recommending and I'm sticking to it."

"What do they teach at BirchBough?" I rolled the new name around in my mouth, grateful for some context beyond Easty-Westy to where I might be going. I could look it up on my Personal Device to get an idea for where I might be headed off to. It was an actual future to hold in my heart, but I was deeply concerned that the Sarge had screwed me.

"It's a bit of a tough school, they will work you harder physically and mentally and emotionally than you would be comfortable with. It's elite, Wheaton. It turns out good, combat ready officers who make a difference in the galaxy. You'd be wasted in some General's secretarial pool and I think that's where you'd go if you were given your druthers."

I really didn't know what to say to him. This wasn't what I had expected. He had screwed me, but only if I agreed with him that I was lazy and that I had been geared up to join a secretarial pool or do some other easy ride of a job that was safe.

He was right. Hadn't I just been folding my socks and filled with trepidation? The idea of actual combat was terrifying. I wanted to curl up with my book and read about fighting, I didn't want to actually be a fighter. But that was crap. If I wasn't brave enough to fight after signing up for the GAF I was using them and I was a hypocrite. I liked to watch but I was too cowardly to get into things myself? Did I think I was too good for combat? Too good for the harder training?

He watched me for awhile, I'm sure my face was an open book to him.

235

"I meant what I said about you being a good girl, Wheaton. I think you can be a good soldier as well. I don't mind my cadets hating me, but I sure would like it if you hated me for the right reasons. You've got to remember that your nature is to be lazy. If you remember that and you push yourself *every time* you catch yourself putting up your hands and walking away to read a book or have an extra long look out a space port... Wheaton, I know that you'll do great things."

He tentatively touched my shoulder and gave it a squeeze.

The next day I was told through official GAF memo that I would be shipped out to BirchBough within the week. I had a lot to think about.

The journey to BirchBough was the easy part but my increasing anxiety was eating me alive. I had run away from home, jettisoning off of Dalton on a lot of momentum that resulted because of my profound sense of injustice and my anger at my father. That had tapered off into the trauma and monotony of basic training and now I was thrust into reality. Only... reality was more waiting.

Here I was, stuck in a ship that wasn't in the best of repair with no clue of how the galaxy was laid out or where I might end up in it. I had researched BirchBough in the week while I had waited to be deployed. This is what my Personal Device had to say about it:

BirchBough Academy

Location: Easty-westy, Beta Quadrant.

BirchBough Academy is a prestigious officer's academy on the training planet of Easty-Westy. It is located in the South Western Hemisphere of the planet and has turned out notable graduates: General Javes Hapton, Colonol Mike Wilcolm, General Habis Davicton (Now Senator Davicton), Major Sarah 'Blaster' Kernowitz, current GAF Chief General Emil Skoda and many other as well.

It is known for tough rules and brutal physical and mental training. It also has a noted Centre for the Arts, started by artist and musician Nick Ollass of Ganymede and former student of BirchBough.

That was all the article said. There were a lot of parts of it that made me nervous and the manipulative 'pep' talk my former CO had given me had since worn off and now I was just all nerves about it once more. The more I thought about it, the more I realized that Sarge probably was a psychopathic sadist and that he was actually, consciously getting off on the fact that my hard earned payment for Officer Academy was going to get wasted on my own failure. If I flunked the training, it was in theory possible to pay for another attempt at another academy, but I had spent every penny I had on this one chance. The more I thought about it the more I worried.

I wasn't even sure if I could pass in a regular, run of the mill officer's academy, let alone a fancy one that was 'tough' and 'brutal'. I worried about it obsessively and tried to spend more time with Stephen or in the bar. Stephen was kind to me and it was nice to be held at night after all this time. I was lonely and Feldmore was right, I had the sads.

Chapter 13 -Leaving

"I have learned that if you must leave a place that you have lived in and loved and where all your yesteryears are buried deep, leave it any way except a slow way, leave it the fastest way you can. Never turn back and never believe that an hour you remember is a better hour because it is dead. Passed years seem safe ones, vanquished ones, while the future lives in a cloud, formidable from a distance."

-Beryl Markham, 'West with the Night'

My sads were interrupted while I was in the bar by the arrival of a policeman and a police woman. They asked to speak to me and took me to a private office, it was about the leaked video of my tearful confession to Howard Donovan, of course.

"We've seen the video on the news and received many phone calls to open an investigation," his tone was resentful and he flipped open his notebook without any sign of invitation to open up to him.

I shifted uncomfortably. The lady cop smiled at me but she seemed uncomfortable as well.

"The video?" I repeated. I didn't mean to play dumb, but I felt dumb.

"The video where you launched a formal complaint with Howard Donovan."

I snorted incredulously. "Launched a formal complaint? Did you watch the whole video? I was drunk. He was drunk, and I didn't know anyone was filming us."

"You were having a discussion in a bar with a Donovan, of course you were being filmed. If you didn't want attention then why were you talking to him?"

The accusations were thick in the air. Why had I dared to think I could talk to someone in the bar? Didn't I know that all Donovans were public property? Why was I trying to get attention?

"I don't want any attention now, and I didn't then."

"Well, we have to take a statement, there is a public outcry."

"I don't know what information you want. If you saw the video then you heard nearly everything that I have to say."

They sat across from the table from me. They both had their arms crossed now. I crossed my own arms and looked back at them. I felt cross and angry that I was being attacked like this. That's how I felt, attacked.

"I'm guessing that you guys have better things to do than to come all the way up to orbit to interrogate me, why don't you just go back. I was drunk and probably didn't know what I was saying."

"Are you retracting your earlier statements?"

"I don't know, maybe, will it end this conversation?"

The door opened and Stephen came in. His brown and red eyes were flashing and his doctor's coat was flapping around him. "Don't answer them, Sasha."

"Who the hell are you?" asked the first cop.

"I'm a friend. A friend of Sasha's and you two aren't," he knelt in front of me to make eye contact.

"Sasha, everything you say about anything to do with this will be recorded and played on the nightly holos. If you retract your statement, they won't take it as though you don't want attention, they will all call you a liar and say that you made up the whole thing."

My eyes filled with tears. I looked up at the ceiling to try to quell them but my voice was cracked.

"But I don't want to press charges against my daddy, I don't want to talk about it. My dad only ever hurt me, and I don't want to do this."

Stephen's translucent eyes blinked at me and he smiled with compassion and stroked my hair. "I know you don't want to do this."
He stood up and placed himself between me and the cops.

"She doesn't want to make a formal statement at this time but reserves the right to do so in the future."

"Will she sign a formal statement to that effect and agree to a formal statement for the holo as well?"

Stephen looked down at me and I knew that I had no choice. I nodded reluctantly.

"She will," he answered for me.

The cops nodded and left the room. I slumped in my chair in dejection. I knew what it meant that the cops had come, I hadn't been watching the news but I was sure that my Dad had been on it at some point. I wondered if he had been arrested and was even more upset at the idea that he might have been fired. How would they survive if he had been fired?

"Do you want to come back to my place, Sasha?"

I nodded and hid my face under his coat against his shirt and smelling his familiar scent. He was still alien to me but he was the first person I had met off of Dalton who voluntarily wanted to spend time with me. He had never had to train me in medicine but he had, whatever his motives might have been, he wanted me and so few people had ever wanted me.

I only had one more day before it was time to leave. I was scared of going to a new place, I was scared of experiencing space travel and HyperDrive for the first time. I was scared of failing officer school and I was scared of being deployed. I missed by home on Dalton for the first time and I was desperately, horribly lonely for Anastasia.

242

"Do you want a glass of wine?"

"So much," I replied. He poured the wine with a flourish. He didn't seem upset, but then, ultimately, he didn't want me to stay so why should he be upset? He had known how long I would be here from the beginning so this wasn't a surprise, not for him and not for me.

"I'm so angry about being filmed. I'm so angry about the way they twist everything I say. I'm just... I'm just, so angry!" I slammed my fist down on its side into the island where we had perched to drink our wine. He nodded sympathetically.

"Yep, I hear you. I really do."

"But...?"

"But, that's the galaxy, Sasha. That's the way it is all over and if you're interesting or if you just cross the path of somebody else who is interesting, you're going to get noticed, and I can guarantee that if you poke your head up at all this is something you better become adept in."

"Talking to the police?"

"Sometimes, mostly, I meant the monitoring. It's happened to me before, more than once. Sasha, I didn't chose a job orbiting a dismal planet like Dalton, I screwed up one too many times on the record and this was a place that I could still work."

"What did you do?"

He looked at me incredulously, judging to see if I was being snide in any way. I felt some of my anger fade, this was a sore spot for Stephen and I had never seen him flinch before in the face of anything.

"I got caught having sex with the wrong somebody. If you're really curious you can search my name on your PD, I guess you've never done that?"

"No, I've never known anyone who would show up in a search."

"Well, you know three people for sure now who will show up on a search, me, Howard Donovan and yourself."

"I'd show up on a search?"

He smiled wryly at me and raised what would have been his eyebrows in a human manner. "You will show up a lot in a search now, my dear girl. You have a gift for being noticed whether you mean to or not, and I know that you don't want to be noticed. I noticed you though, and it's going to keep happening so you better resign yourself to it and learn some tactics to deal with it or it'll wreck you."

I took another drink of wine. Overwhelmed was only a smidge of the feelings that were consuming me. Stephen poured me another glass, I had emptied my first glass.

"Suggestions?"

"Suggestions? For surviving it, you mean? Well, I would suggest that you start off by accepting that this is going to happen. You have a couple of connections, me and Donovan, use us if you have to. That's the only way to survive being in the center of one of these spectacles, that and if it comes to it, hire a publicist. If you can't afford one, send me a message, I'll help you if I can."

I didn't know what to say to that and I murmured a thank you. He changed the subject and when I spent the night in his clam shell bed once more, neither one of us was surprised.

The next morning I showered off the inevitable slime and Stephen gave me the antidote to his venom. He recorded me after my hair dried giving a carefully thought out statement that he helped me write.

'I would like to state formally at this time that I am not currently prepared to give a report to the police or other law enforcement agencies about the private conversation recorded with Howard Donovan. This was not a public statement nor a formal statement and I'm under no legal obligation to pursue charges.'

He turned off his PD. I looked at him nervously, hoping for some sign of approval from him. "It's fine, Sasha. You can always change your mind now if you want to bring up charges and the rest of it is up to whether anyone wants to bother running this on Primetime. I'm hoping for your sake that interest has waned enough that the police will just hold onto your tape to forestall any legal obligations."

"I don't see what legal obligations they would have."

"It's all very complicated but it boils down to the fact that they heard about what happened with you and your dad gives them an obligation to do something about it. You could hire a lawyer and sue them if they didn't."

"Oh."

"Yes, oh."

Stephen delivered the recording of the holograph of me giving my statement. It seemed anticlimactic after how attacked and fearful the confrontation the day before had made me feel.

I spent my last night orbiting Dalton in my bed in the dorm. It was weird being in there with Midge and Guido, the only two in my room who were still there. I felt disconnected from Midge, I wasn't going to see her again, maybe ever. I hoped I would see Guido again, but I was also embarrassed still by our shared training and failures. There was something sordid in what we had experienced together and in a way, I wanted nothing more than to get away from all of them, as far as I could.

We boarded the ship that would take us away the next morning, me and Guido, and it was the end of something, that was the only thing that I knew for sure.

Chapter 14 -HyperDrive

"We live in a society exquisitely dependent on science and technology, in which hardly anyone knows anything about science and technology."

-Carl Sagan

The ship was much different from the space station. The very first thing about it was that it had a destination and a movement to it, and that was before it entered HyperDrive.

I had been afraid of HyperDrive ever since I had thoroughly understood it. Your atoms spend quite a bit of time being in an 'other' state of reality and when you reassemble on the other end you are actually made up of slightly different atoms than the ones you started off with. What happened to your original atoms? Nobody seemed to have an answer for that.

We were warned by the pilot over the intercom before we slipped into HyperDrive and we all went to our beds and were strapped down for the duration of the time that we fell into the Hyperpathway slipstream. It wasn't a particularly dangerous maneuver but some coordination was required to make sure you didn't land in the path of another ship. That could cause a serious accident in HyperDrive. You would have to have very bad timing to run right into someone but there were cases of it happening.

As soon as we headed to HyperDrive there was very little to look out the windows at, just the glow of the hyperpathway and streaks that might have been stars or might have been more light. I didn't like the feel of HyperDrive and sliding into it left me feeling disquieted.

I only had one other roommate, a girl named Tish who seemed friendly at first but increasingly made me feel uncomfortable with every passing day. I wondered if it was cabin fever or a bad reaction to the HyperDrive. I didn't believe that it was the HyperDrive, there was something... antagonistic even in her friendliness that made me feel like a fox at bay. Something was wrong with her and most of the time I was sequestered in our room with her. I wasn't feeling very social and Stephen's warnings about sticking out and attracting attention had left me feeling dejected and unfriendly.

HyperDrive was giving me nightmares and there were few introverted activities that were available without communication link up with the GAGA or GAF VoidNet being available, that was yet another downside of HyperDrive. I only had the one book with me, Arthur and the Knights of Camelot, and I read it even though there were parts that made me cry quietly into my pillow. Even crying is boring after awhile and I finally decided to go into the main room where everyone else was and try to act a bit more social.

The nightmares were the main reason why I didn't want to interact with anyone. I found even bunking with Tish to be ever more exhausting every day. She was always very concerned by my nightmares and generally was always asking after me and if I was 'okay'. That got really old in a hurry.

She was making me nervous even though she hadn't actually done anything to me. I was worried that the nightmares and my first trip in HyperDrive were making me paranoid. I asked the bored ship doctor if paranoia was a possible side effect of HyperDrive and he just shrugged and asked if I needed a prescription filled. I went back to my room.

There wasn't a lot else to do on the ship except to doodle and to sleep if I wasn't going to be social. I fell asleep and found myself back in the desert again.

This was my HyperDrive dream:

I woke up in the desert but I knew it was the desert more by its feel. I was alone in a large house. Some of the windows were boarded over and others were left wide open, they didn't have any glass in them or a screen or anything. There was a wind blowing and I was afraid.

The house had thick walls that looked to me as though they had been sculpted of sand. I had a knowledge that I was looking for my family, but they weren't anywhere to be found. I was scared to go outside, because of the wind, but also because of something else that I couldn't put my finger on. My clothing was strange and when I caught a glimpse of myself I blushed. I looked beautiful and I was embarrassed by the kohl lined eyes that looked back at me, huge and brown. Something had been done to them to make them look more hazel or green than they actually are.

In my nightmare I explore the house, afraid to go outside, then, as I am standing on the stairwell and looking around the atrium of the house the sky goes black. There is a change in pressure and my throat catches as though my neck is being squeezed. I freeze in place, one hand half raised to ward off something... Then the windows blow in.

That's what I thought at first. That the spray and particulates are broken glass, it takes me a minute to realize that it's sand spraying in through the open windows and even the gaps in the boards have been covered over. I crouch and run down the stairs bent low. The spray of cutting sand continued relentlessly.

I ran without thought, suddenly knowing the house. The cellar, I had to get to the cellar. There weren't any windows in the cellar! I slammed and barred the heavy wooden door behind me. It was solid and reinforced with metal that went across even the hinges were interconnected with the metal. It was safe. I ran down the stone steps that were worn in the middle with little scoops taken out from so many feet using them for so long. It was quiet down there and I felt a deep sense of relief to be away from the blowing sand and the blackness in the air and the roar of the wind.

It was dark in the cellar but someone had oddly left several oil lamps burning on their sconces on the walls. The cellar was dim with the shadows of shelves and barrels and smelled like dried figs and spices. It was warm and dry and felt safe. There were some rugs hung up on the walls. I looked at the elaborate, snaking designs and in the flickering lamplight.

They seemed to writhe around like a cluster of serpents.

I was beginning to feel lost when I heard the sound of rocks being tumbled behind me and the soft grunts of a man moving things and trying to be quiet. The noises were coming from behind one of the tapestries. I saw with alarm that the tapestry was being moved around. Whoever was behind the tapestry was just about to break free!

I looked for a weapon but everything was either too big or too small. I found a small keg and hefted it in the air, and moved closer to the sound. That had been one of the hardest things for me to learn in basic training: to go towards a threat when it was called for. I forced myself forward, imagining as I had learned to do that it was Anastasia who was in danger rather than myself, that this time I was playing Lancelot. That always got my feet moving.

I lifted the keg and was prepared to smash without questioning when something stopped me. Maybe it was just caution but it felt more like intuition. My eyes were wide with anxiety and I felt weak in my knees when a head covered in long, red hair pushed past the edge of the tapestry with a cough and a small cloud of dust. He pushed his hair out of his eyes and smiled sheepishly at me, his smile only briefly fading as he glanced at my lofted keg.

In my dream, I thought I was going to faint. It was Verily Wrought.

251

I woke up on my bunk, Tish asked if I was okay and I irritatedly asked her if she ever slept. She replied that I didn't need to be so cross and then I rolled over and went back to sleep. I really really wish that I would stop having dreams about Verily Wrought. At least that was just a very real dream as opposed to an out and out nightmare. It left me hurting in my heart and wishing that I had something. It was a painful longing and I couldn't find a way to stop it.

The next day I determined that I would go out and meet some other people. Trish was driving me insane.

There were a lot of people on the ship who weren't from Dalton. They felt strange to me. Rowdy. I was coming back from the doctor's and she stood up quickly when I walked into the room. I narrowed my eyes - She looked guilty. I wished Dr. Johnson were here... I had to block that thought from my mind. He was a wonderful mentor though and it had always been such a boon to have him there when I had a question on my mind.

I thought briefly of Howard, and even of Sarge, someone I could talk to... Sarge didn't usually fit that bill in my mind. The talk he had had with me had settled in my mind into a pleasant experience with a bit of space and time between it. I had to have faith that he was right to believe in me and right to think I would do well at Birch Bough. Stephen had told me that Sarge had likely had the conversation in part because of the influence of the media. I didn't understand how that could be but he assured me that these things had deeper consequences and a larger effect on people than imagination allowed.

Feeling bothered, I went into the lunch/game room and hoped that i would find some people who I could bond with, I was mostly hoping to find Guido and had gotten over my shame enough to miss him as a friend. It's so stupid. I had joined the Galactic Armed Forces, I had paid money for officer's school. It was an honour to be able to go.

Why wouldn't my brain ever let me be happy with anything I did? How about my heart? Would my heart ever let me be happy? With that thought my heart surged in pain and I remembered the gentle look in dream Verily's large blue eyes. Why had I set myself up for heartbreak in life?

I had seen the lunch/recreation room on my various sojourns around the 'Space Blaster' before but every time I had thought about going in at the last minute I had changed my mind and diverted to the instant dispenser instead. It was loud in there.

Today I was resolved. I went in for breakfast, glad to not have to eat breakfast under Trish's watchful eye for the first time on the voyage. She seemed outgoing and I would see her coming down the hallway with this fellow or that and she would laugh loudly and flick her shoulder length pink hair behind her shoulder flirtatiously and then walk her tray back to our room. I wished she would eat in the lunchroom. I had learned to value privacy during basic training and the general vibe there had been much more friendly than this. I would hear Trish laughing and it sounded mean. Sometimes I thought I heard my name before some of the mean laughter but I couldn't let myself think of that. That road wasn't any good for anyone.

My heart clenched nervously and my hands were moist when I pushed the door open. A part of me expected the entire room to go silent but it didn't. I picked up a tray and went to the end of the line. The warm food smelled good after days of machine vended food. I found a spot at the far end of one of the tables.
-*

It seemed like most of the crew of the Space Blaster was mostly male and very large. They consumed two trays at once in some cases. I felt incredibly insignificant and simultaneously conspicuous. I was relieved when after a few shufflings to make sure that they had given me enough room that they all went back to their meals.

It wasn't a very large ship and I spotted Guido sandwiched between a guy three times his size and the wall and went over to where he was. I was absurdly happy to see him, a little shrimp like me amidst what seemed at that moment to be a ship of giants.

"Hey, Sasha... you survived HyperDrive."

I grimaced. "Barely. I've been having wicked strange dreams. Have you had anything like that happen to you?"

He shook his head. "Not that, but my stomach's been upset. I keep coming here to eat and it's beginning to seem pretty pointless."

He was poking the food on his plate disconsolately and he did look kind of green. He pushed the plate a bit away from him and tried to find a place in the room where someone wasn't shoveling food in their mouth to fix his gaze on. I couldn't help but laugh a bit at him. "You really shouldn't be in here if it's that bad for you. Why don't you eat in your room? That's what I've been doing."

"I can't stand my bunkmates and I've got five of them in my room. I mostly wait until the pinball machine is free and kill some time playing it. I can't wait to get to Easty-Westy."

"Me too. My roommate is, well, I don't know, I guess I can't stand her either, but mostly I think I've got cabin fever."

"Worse than snuggling up with us lot in the arctic? I find that hard to believe. You only have one roommate?"

"Only one, she's, I don't know, sometimes you just get a weird feeling about someone, even when they seem to be really nice."

Guido smiled over my shoulder and I turned around to see Trish standing behind me. She was hard to miss with her pale pink hair and her pink bubble gum and her white lipstick.

"Oh, hi, Trish... Trish, this is Guido, Guido, Trish."

I crammed my bun into my mouth and looked down at my plate. It really seems like anytime that I talk about someone behind their back I get massively caught out about it. I tried to remember the last thing I had said and if I had said anything really bad or if I just felt this guilty.

She popped her gum and looked down her nose at me, which was normal because she was standing behind me and I was sitting but I had the impression with her that she really was looking down at me.

Guido grinned and raised his eyebrows at Trish who looked back at him with her cool pale blue eyes. He looked at me questioningly.

"Trish is my roommate."

"Oh, jeez, goood to meet you, I know Sasha from the way back. Way back to the start of basic training. Are you from Dalton, Trish."

"Hell, no. That crap planet? I'm from Weenus."

"Oh, Weenus, I've heard of your planet. Coal mining and fossils and diamonds, right? Kind of underpopulated from what I understand but I've heard you have some great clubs in some of your major cities."

She was still guarded but taken aback by his knowledge. I could understand that now having learned that 'Dalton' and 'ignorant hick' were apparently synonomous. She didn't know that Guido was from Old Earth and had the benefit of being decidedly more galactic than myself or the others from Dalton. I smiled, she had made it sound like Weenus was practically Brandenburg for opulence and position in the galaxy.

"Yes, we do have, um, a lot of good clubs."

Guido was leaning back against the wall and smiling the smiled that he used when he wanted to be charming with someone but not for entirely kind reasons. His next words verified my assumption.

"A lot of good clubs that you've never been to. I bet you're from some little rural place? Plus, you're too young to be club hopping. I bet your parents wouldn't let you out past your curfew and that's why you joined the GAF. Am I right? Now you're angrily on your way to Easty-Westy, huh, wow. Good for you."

He stood up with he tray. I didn't know what Trish had done to offend him deeply enough for him to come out swinging like that but I had to bite the insides of my cheeks hard to suppress my laughter. He leaned down and whispered where to find him if I needed anything and then left the mess, weaving around the others deftly with his head up.

"You know him? Who does he think he is except the rudest person anywhere."

I still couldn't talk. I was trying not to laugh and I also couldn't think of anything political or nice to say to her about it. I was swept up and punchy from Guido's energy and I wanted to get a punch or two in myself but there was still a long trip ahead of us so I just crammed the rest of my bun in my mouth and shrugged, trying not to make any sort of eye contact with Trish as I did so.

She set her tray down and continued with narrowed eyes. "Did you come here to meet him today? It's *weird* to me that you would come here for like the first time ever and find him here."

I was trying to finish my lunch as quickly as I could now. I answered with a full mouth and another shrug. Quick as a viper she yanked my try away from me and threw it on the ground behind me. It clattered loudly and a lot of people in our radius turned to look at us. Trish didn't apologize or even seem to notice the regard at us. She sat, squeezed in beside me on the bench, staring at me with her jaw. I got up and picked up the tray and put it on the tray wash stand. I got out of there and went back to our room.

It was 'our' room and it was a flaw in my thinking to think that this was a safe spot to retreat to. I was confused by the way Trish had acted and hurt and embarrassed by the way she had made me feel. I hadn't had a lot of friends when I went to school and I had never had enough experiences to figure it out.

Trish came back to our room awhile later. A boy walked her to the door and they came in and made out on her bed. I went and had a shower and by the time I had come back he was gone again. Trish had always seemed nice before but now I felt like everything I said was walking along the edge of a steel trap about to spring shut on me.

"Did you like him?"

"Like him?"

"Timontin, the guy who was just in here. Did you think he was cute?"

"I didn't look at him too closely and you guys were kind of, um, busy."

"Oh, is that what the kids these days are calling it, being 'busy'. Tim and I were *making out,* Sasha, that's different from

258

being busy. Do you understand what I mean?"

"Why are you talking to me like that?"

"Like what?"

"Like I'm an idiot."

She flopped back on the bed. I noticed she had a small hickey on her neck. "Only because you act like an idiot, Sasha."

I turned away from her and put my clothes away. I started to think of anyplace I could go to get away from her and get some quiet time in my own head as she went on.

"You're such a little kid. That's why I have to treat you like you're an idiot. Do you think that boy you were sitting with liked you? Is that what you think?"

"Leave Guido alone, you don't know anything about him."

"Oooh, you *like* him, don't you. You think he likes you too?"

She sat up again, she was very twitchy, she always was, it was one of the things about her that made me uneasy.

"Sasha, now tell me the truth, do you let that boy do things to you? Do you let him touch you?"

My face drained of blood and I gaped at her. She nodded smugly.

259

"I thought as much. You do let him touch you. You're a very dirty girl, Sash, I guess your daddy taught you that much."

At that point I lost all cohesion and thought. I had had to talk about the matter somewhat rationally to the police and to Stephen, I had unloaded myself to Howard Donovan which had of course been what had let all the galaxy in on my confession. But in all the time my secret had been on the loose, I had never ever been openly mocked about it before.

I fell into what is referred to as a 'blackout rage' or in the old old days, 'berserking'.

I attacked her like I was a cat, my fingers extended into claws. There wasn't a thought in my head at that moment, I had only the idea of hurting her physically the way she had just hurt me in my soul.

I clawed a strip off of her face and pulled her hair, she hauled back and punched me in the jaw.

It hurt like all hell and it almost had the effect of sobering me up, but then I saw her smug smile and I screamed and attacked her again. I can sincerely tell you the same thing I told ship security, that I had no idea how long this went on for.

Someone heard us, plus our room was monitored with security cameras. Do I need to spell out for you what happened next?

I was put into a holding cell since it was clear on the tape that I was the first one to make physical contact with Trish, she was sent back to our room and locked in. We both had to make a formal statement that would be filed officially with GAF HQ upon our exit from HyperDrive, a statement that would lead to a reprimand and a permanent blot on both of our records, but especially mine.

Then the inevitable happened, somebody sold the security footage once we were out of HyperDrive and I arrived at Easty-Westy with a chipped tooth, a broken nose, a still healing black eye and my face once more on the evening news.

It was an inauspicious start to my career at BirchBough and Trish and I had spent the entire rest of the trip together. When I got back to our room I discovered that she had gone through my things and had stolen my blue sapphire. She said that I owed her for scratching her face.

I apologized through gritted teeth for scratching her face and asked her for the sapphire back again. She denied having it and I had to go back to security and ask them to run the tape to prove that she had stolen it.

Security had come and demanded she give it back to me as you could see her take it as clear as day on the coloured images. She had cried and screamed that it was hers now and that we all owed her before throwing it back in my face.

Her humour flared and quieted through the rest of the trip but we both looked pretty rough for the entire thing. That didn't stop her from bringing boy after boy back to our room. I didn't care about that too much except that she would giggle with them and whisper about me in a voice too loud to ignore while I sat on my bed and many nights I was chased out of our room to go and play pinball in the mess with Guido or to sit with him

261

somewhere else if he wasn't too busy.

That was also how I heard from him that at least I wasn't going to be alone at BirchBough.

"I found out about the change of plans pretty much right before we left. Clemdale was all filled up and so Sarge decided to try a shot for BirchBough and I guess they thought I was a good fit."

"Do you know anything about it? I'm kind of petrified about it."

"Petrified? Why?"

"I heard it's hard. I only had the money to put up a fee for it once and I don't want to lose it and be an enlisted man. That, that would just be bad."

"I understand, but Sasha, you're going to do great. I mean, look at you, you're a fighter!"

I laughed ruefully. Neither one of us fully understood how good the chances were that when we dropped out of HyperDrive it wouldn't just be the people on this little ship who knew about what a fighter I was.

Disembarking with my gear at Birch Bough I saw Trish glaring at me and I was relived to have Guido here. I had successfully made my first real enemy in life and I still didn't understand that it had all happened because I had a friend in Guido and she was jealous to be outside of that. We hugged a hug of friendship just before a PA boomed out the announcement that would be the first one I would hear at BirchBough.

"Cadet Sasha Wheaton to General Haber's office *immediately.* Cadet Sasha Wheaton."

I knew by Guido's expression what the announcement meant.

I was in big trouble.

...To Be Continued.

www.ingramcontent.com/pod-product-compliance
Lightning Source LLC
Chambersburg PA
CBHW071829020726
47502CB00004B/1296